Everybody loves
The Last Kids on Earth series!

"TERRIFYINGLY FUN! Max Brallier's *The Last Kids on Earth* delivers big thrills and even bigger laughs." —JEFF KINNEY, author of the #1 *New York Times* bestseller *Diary of a Wimpy Kid*

★ "A GROSS-OUT GOOD TIME with surprisingly nuanced character development."
—*School Library Journal*, starred review

★ "Classic ACTION-PACKED, monster-fighting fun." —*Kirkus Reviews*, starred review

★ "SNARKY END-OF-THE-WORLD FUN."
—*Publishers Weekly*, starred review

"The likable cast, lots of adventure, and GOOEY, OOZY MONSTER SLIME GALORE keep the pages turning." —*Booklist*

"Jack is a fantastic narrator . . . Young zombie fans will rejoice in this new series that has all the oozing (by the zombies) and heroism (by the kids) that they could hope for."
—*Bulletin of the Center for Children's Books*

"HILARIOUS and FULL OF HEART." —*Boys' Life*

"*The Last Kids on Earth* is a BLAST."

—Powell's Books

"I would recommend *The Last Kids on Earth* for PEOPLE WHO LIKE VIDEO GAMES because it is equally as fast-paced."   —*The Guardian*

"It's hard to find something unexpected to do with zombies, but this clever mix of black-and-white drawings and vivid prose brings new life to the living dead."   —Common Sense Media

"The MONSTERS IN THIS BOOK just beg to COME ALIVE."   —Parenting Chaos

"One-part SWISS FAMILY ROBINSON, and one-part WALKING DEAD, Max Brallier and Doug Holgate's well-imagined book is sure to appeal to readers with big imaginations."

—Reading Nook Reviews

"The NEXT HOT READING ADVENTURE for reluctant readers or for anyone looking for a fast-paced, humorous adventure."   —Guys Lit Wire

Winner of the Texas Bluebonnet Award

THE LAST KIDS ON EARTH

and the COSMIC BEYOND

MAX BRALLIER & DOUGLAS HOLGATE

VIKING

VIKING
Penguin Young Readers
An imprint of Penguin Random House LLC
375 Hudson Street
New York, New York 10014

First published in the United States of America by Viking,
an imprint of Penguin Random House LLC, 2018

Text copyright © 2018 by Max Brallier
Illustrations copyright © 2018 by Douglas Holgate

LIBRARY OF CONGRESS CATALOGING-IN-PUBLICATION DATA IS AVAILABLE.
ISBN 9780425292082

Printed in the USA

10   9   8   7   6   5   4   3   2   1

Book design by Jim Hoover   Set in Cosmiqua Com and Carrotflower

For my Lila Bean.

—M. B.

For Turtle and Panda.

—D. H.

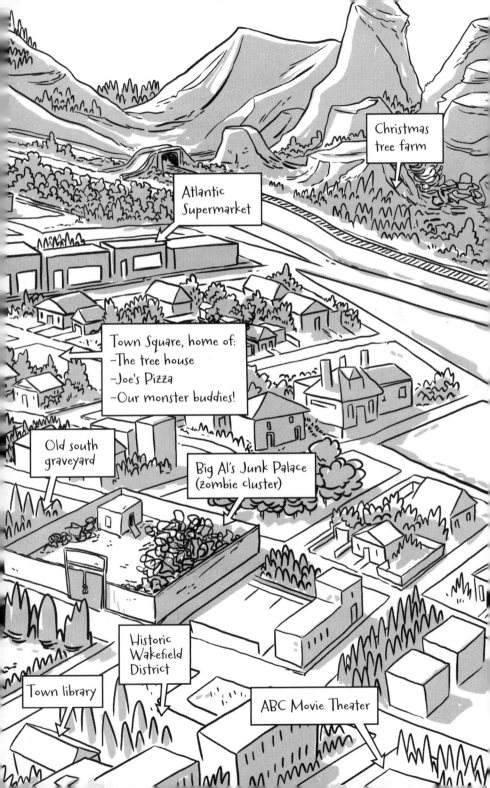

chapter one

So, we are about to be astro-blasted. Catapulted and *launched*. Propelled off the roof of our tree house by something called the Sled-Shot.

Why? Why load ourselves into a massive slingshot and blast ourselves off the roof?

Why did some old guy climb Mount Everest?
BECAUSE IT'S THERE!!!

Actually, that's not the reason at all. The
Sled-Shot was of course not just "there." My
best friend, Quint Baker, built it.

"Quint, are you sure this is safe?" I ask.

He thinks for a moment, then says, "No. But I'm not *not* sure."

"What's the matter? A little nervous, Jack?"

That's my buddy-crush, June Del Toro. I know she's teasing me, but I actually do feel kind of queasy. Usually, I'm super gung-ho about all things action, no matter the danger. But not this.

I give the Sled-Shot a final look before I slide in. "Quint, this looks like a weapon for medieval siege warfare! Or for defending a castle against an army of orcs! Or for storming a castle *with* an army of orcs! This would be helpful if we were under siege, but we're very much *not* under siege."

June grins. "We are under *snow*."

"Not the same," I say. "Not even kind of sort of the same."

"But *they* think it is," June says.

They are the monsters who are our friends. The dozen or so monsters up here with us in the tree house, helping us prepare for blastoff. And the many other monsters down below, in Wakefield Town Square.

And it's true. The monsters are probably more worried about the snow than they would be about an army of orcs. They are not inspiring confidence. . . .

Hey! No one's got dibs on my monster buddy Rover and definitely no one is sleeping in my bed! I glare at Skaelka. She's the one with the big ax.

My big buddy Dirk Savage—the final member of our foursome of friends—says, "Enough talk! We're going. Equip helmets."

"Helmets equipped!" we respond.

"Equip inflatable donut rafts!" Quint shouts.

"Equipped!" my buddies say.

"Equipped!" I say. But that's only partly true.

See, Quint designed instant-inflate donut rafts. They're basically airbags for your body. But I'm Jack Sullivan! I don't need that! Quint's a worrier, though, so I agreed to wear it.

What I *didn't* tell him is that I filled mine with delicious snacks! I mean, honestly—what are the odds I'm going to need an instant-inflate raft? Not high. But the odds I'm gonna want delicious snacks? WAY HIGH. Plus, I get to walk around looking less lame than my buds—see?

"You may fire when ready!" Quint says to the monsters. There's a big grin on his face. It is the grin of someone who has always wanted to say "you may fire when ready" and just finally got his chance.

Skaelka cocks back the sled. The tree house rattles. I hear whirring, I hear clanking, I hear gears turning. This is happening and there's no stopping it. And then . . .

My stomach doesn't *just* flip. My stomach does a jackknife, a cannonball, and follows it with an atomic belly flop. We fly through the air for so long I feel like E.T. And . . .

SMASH!

We crash through the roof of a Chinese takeout joint, barrel through Wendy's, explode through the Blue Point Diner. A total sled rampage.

Ahead of us is a truck, tilted on its side, covered in ice. It looks like something out of a racing game.

And I see something else just past the truck. A monster.

A monster, standing massive in the swirling snow, waiting for us. A single, giant fist rests on the ground. The monster leans forward. It snarls, and—

Actually—y'know what. HOLD UP!

Now is a good time to explain a few things. Like, y'know—WHY we are sailing through the sky in a death sled. In fact, it's time for a real-deal recap. . . .

PREVIOUSLY ON . . . THE LAST KIDS ON EARTH:
It all started seven months ago—with the Monster
Apocalypse. Interdimensional portal doors opened
above the earth—like this . . .

Those portals flung *crazy stuff* into our world:
massive monsters, creepy creatures, and slimy
shrieking strangeness. Plus—and this is big—
the *horrible zombie plague* that turned most of
humanity undead.

There are good monsters and there are bad
monsters. The good monsters are now our buddies!
They live in our little 'burb—Wakefield—in the
Town Square.

The bad monsters are *bad*. They worship the
diabolical ultra-villain Ŗeżżóch the Ancient,
Destructor of Worlds. But, good news . . .

Ṛeżżőcħ is still stuck in the other dimension! He tried to come to *our* world to do bad stuff 'cause that's what inter-dimensional villains do. But we shut down his plan!

For a while, life was great! Me and my buddies and our monster pals battled evil and had fun. But a month back, everything changed. . . .

We found a RADIO.

And that radio picked up a broadcast from OTHER HUMANS. . . .

Hello. We are a large group of humans who have survived the Monster Apocalypse. We are in New York City, located inside the Statue of Liberty. All are welcome. . . .

So, just last week, we were like: ROAD TRIP! Destination: NYC. We packed up our monster-battling truck, Big Mama, and we were about to start our journey. But then . . .

A snowstorm hit. A snowfall so strong it might have been sent by the ice lords themselves!

This nasty nor'easter trapped us and put our journey on hold. That didn't actually bother *me* at all, 'cause I felt bad leaving our monster buddies, anyway. See, the concept of snow was *totally new* to the monsters.

And it freaked them out.

Big time.

So, we were TRAPPED and the monsters were FREAKED.

And I mean—Earth is my dimension. My world. And I didn't like the monsters being afraid of the snow—I felt like a bad host!

So I was like, "I will PROVE that snow is nothing to be afraid of! I'll prove it in the most death-defying and dramatic way possible! We'll attack the snow head-on—by sledding! INSANE sledding—like ROCKETING OURSELVES FROM THE TREE HOUSE IN A SLED!"

First, we winterized the tree house. Take a peek. . . .

The biggest winter addition was the Sled-Shot. See, the first rule of life after the Monster Apocalypse is that *there are zero rules,* so you can and *should* do everything in a totally ridiculous fashion!

Catapult

Zip line (great for last-minute escapes)

The Sled-Shot

Actually, I lied—the first rule is don't get bitten by a zombie and also don't get eaten by a monster—but after that, it's the rule about over-the-top ridiculousness.

So, we climbed into the Sled-Shot, our monster buddies flung us, we went sailing *way too far and way too fast*, and now . . .

BACK TO THE PRESENT AWFUL AND SCARY MONSTER MOMENT.

"Dudes!" June cries out. "We are on a direct collision course with that one-armed monster's mouth!"

"I know it, I know it!" I say.

Rapid-fire, I analyze the situation, seeing every possible maneuver and attack. I think it's a skill I picked up from watching too many movies, reading too many graphic novels, and playing too many video games. . . .

So as we sail toward the great monster's maw, I realize the courageous, valiant, lion-hearted action that must be taken. . . .

"OVERBOARD!" I scream. "FLEE! EMBRACE YOUR INNER COWARD, BUDDIES!"

"But my vehicle, Jack!" Quint cries out.

Quint's brain is *not* an action hero brain. It's a different, awesome brain. But he simply cannot process abandoning something he's worked so hard on. He doesn't worry about the imminent death.

So I have to worry about it for him. I grip his sweater and—

SNAP!

17

chapter two

Overboard was the right decision.

There's a *gulp*—and the great beast's belly rumbles. The sled has been swallowed. Two seconds later and he would've swallowed *us*, too.

I hate sledding.

Nah, sledding rules. We just did bad at it.

Maybe a death-defying sled jump was **not** the best way to start off the winter. . . .

You guys didn't even use your instant-inflate tubes!

A monstrous roar cuts through the air.

"C'mon!" June shouts. She yanks me to my feet. Dirk pulls Quint from the snow, and we race out onto a wide street.

Snow whips through the air, like I'm inside a snow globe. It's like when you have to get up in the middle of the night to pee but you can't see *anything*. Only then, the worst-case scenario is you fall into an open toilet. Here the worst-case scenario is—y'know—death by monster.

CRUNCH!
CRUNCH!
CRUNCH!

Our bodies bounce. The snow-cracking CRUNCHES are deafening. The monster's coming after us, but I only see its huge stomping legs.

"Guys! We need to get to cover!" I shout.

I'm using my Louisville Slicer like a cane, staggering forward while poking around. And that is *not* what the Louisville Slicer is for. It's for battling monsters! It's my ultimate weapon.

I slayed Blarg with the Louisville Slicer! I battled Thrull with it! I sliced the lassos that held the King Wretch with it!

BLARG:
Big, brutal beast.

THRULL:
Man-monster! Undercover traitor monster!

KING WRETCH:

This dude gave me weird dream-visions and then his chest opened so Ṛeżżöch could talk to me and, yeah, it was nuts.

THE LOUISVILLE SLICER:

My radical weapon.
It did damage to all these bad dudes.

I mean, that bat is basically my lightsaber!

CRUNCH!

The monster stomps grow louder. Up ahead, I see an opening—like the mouth of a cave. . . . What the—where *are* we? I thought we were in the suburbs, but now we've stumbled upon some sort of cave situation?

"Whoa, whoa," Dirk says. "Could be frost giants. Frost giants live in caves—learned that from *Conan the Barbarian*."

June sighs. "Dudes, *really*? It's not a cave! It's the car wash!"

Another *CRUNCH!*

"In we go!" I say, and we race into the car wash tunnel.

Even inside, the cold is crippling. Quint's teeth are chattering. We really need to upgrade our winter outfits—if we don't, hypothermia might take us down before a monster—

RAWRRR!

The monster's howl slices through the car wash, bouncing off the walls. "The big guy found us!" June cries. It's at the entrance.

The beast's hot breath warms the air, turning the car wash tunnel into a humid haze.

Through the mist, I see the monster: a giant, one-armed beast with a single fistacular paw. One massive . . .

-MEATHOOK!-

This monster—*Meathook*—bends down. It peers into the car wash tunnel.

And that's when I see there's something *on top* of the beast. A figure wearing a dark cloak that snaps in the wind.

I gulp.

We carefully inch forward, peeking out around the tunnel's corner. We watch the figure's arm raise and clasp the cloak.

A hood is pulled back.

And then—

"Whoa!" I exclaim.

"Oh my," Quint says.

June stammers, "It's—it's—it's a person. A human!"

chapter three

This is monumentally unexpected. This woman atop the monster is the first other human we've seen. Until we heard that radio broadcast, we didn't even know other humans still *existed*!

June grabs my sleeve and twists it tight. Her eyes are high-beam wide.

You think she knows about the human settlement in New York?

Maybe she has her own settlement. One with real houses and other kids that aren't three dorky boys.

Let's initiate communication.

"Hold up, hold up!" I say. "This human's intentions may not be great. She is, y'know, *riding a giant fanged beast*!"

June shakes her head. "You ride Rover! He's a giant fanged beast!"

"Maybe *technically* he's a beast—but really he's just a big fluffy monster-dog!" I say. "This monster here looks like something out of a demon's nightmare! Plus, it ate Quint's sled!"

Quint is jittery beside me. I can almost hear the wheels in his brain spinning away with curiosity and excitement—*clink, clink, clink.*

And like that, he goes to make contact. . . .

From the tunnel, we watch the human eye Quint. Then the monster tilts its head. Then—

HARRRUGH!

The monster raises its fist, and I can see what's coming—Pancake Quint. "Crud!" I scream as I race out to grab my friend.

"I miscalculated!" Quint cries out. "That human is a villainess!"

"No kidding!" I yell, pulling him across the snow. "And that monster's a meathook!"

Meathook's fist comes slamming down, snow erupting, throwing us back into the car wash.

The monster's fist opens and it reaches into the tunnel. It swipes and thrashes. Luckily, the arm is not long enough to reach us.

And he's not pleased about it.

But then—

Footsteps outside. *Human* footsteps. Suddenly—

POP! SIZZLE! An electrical hum. Harsh fluorescent overhead lights flash on.

"THE CAR WASH! IT'S ALIVE!" screams Dirk.

The automatic car wash conveyor suddenly jolts us forward. . . .

So, I've been through a drive-through car wash many times. Always in a car, naturally. And I thought it would be just *so goofy and fun* to go through one on foot. Not true.

The nozzles are as strong as fire hoses! Snow, dirt, and gunk fly off us.

A roar echoes down the length of the car wash tunnel. I see the monster appear at the exit. It is now waiting for us, where the conveyor ends. Our conveyor belt of *cleanliness* is now a conveyor belt of *doom*, carrying us on a deadly path to a fang-filled mouth.

"Run back! The other way!" I shout.

But the whole thing is moving too fast—it's like trying to walk down an up escalator. Our only choice is to embrace the conveyor!

Massive brushes whack us! Then we're dried off—hit with high-pressure air and smacked with huge strips of towel.

We race down the belt. Every step is like Flash-style hyperspeed. We burst through a big wall of flapping thingies and then the conveyor belt *hurls* us out of the tunnel.

My feet slide across black ice. I spin past Meathook, managing to stay upright. In an instant, I've lost track of my buddies.

I reach out, feeling for something I can use as cover. My hand finds metal. Hmmm . . . *smells* like a Dumpster. I yank open the Dumpster lid and dive inside. It clangs shut behind me.

I hold my breath, because I don't want the monster or the Villainess to hear me, but also because the Dumpster smells like death.

I grip the Louisville Slicer tight against my chest. I expect a long, dramatic moment to pass—with breathing, and terror, and waiting—but it's *only an instant*!

YANK! The Dumpster lid is *ripped* open, and something awful enters. . . .

KRAK!

Meathook's gray-purple tongue snaps and smacks me across the face. I half expect it to follow that with a French kiss of death. Instead, small, fleshy slivers of tongue wrap around the Louisville Slicer!

I throw my other hand around my weapon's handle. Meathook *pulls*—a vicious, terrible *jerk*. My arms are nearly ripped from the sockets, like I insulted a Wookiee, and then—

"Give that back!" I demand, as I crash to the ground. "That's *my weapon*, I named it *the Louisville Slicer*, and it's *not for you*!"

CRACK!

I see June, beneath the monster, whacking its leg with her flagpole spear. But she might as well be hitting it with a very long pretzel rod, because it does nothing.

Atop the monster, glaring down, is the Villainess. She chuckles, Meathook's tongue snaps, and my blade is thrown upward, flipping end over end, until—

GRAB!

"Jack, forget about it!" June shouts.

She pulls me away. And as she does, I see that the enemy has dropped something. A card on the ground. I scoop it up, as—

SPLATOOT!

The monster spits, but it is *not* a monstrous puke-wad that flies from this brute's mouth. It's . . .

OUR SLED!

It crashes to the snowy ground, flips, rolls, and completely *shatters*.

Quint whimpers. "My creation . . . it is no more."

A screen of snow is kicked up, giving us enough cover to race down the street. After three blocks I pause to look back. Through the haze of snow, I see bits of the monster. One second, just white flakes—and then the dark shadow of the thing.

And the Villainess.

On top, holding my blade.

She must know we're still watching—because she suddenly *screams*. But the words that come out—they're—they're not *human*.

I gasp. We all do. That's the language
of Ṛeżżǒch the Ancient, Destructor of Worlds.

chapter four

The whole walk back to town, our heads are spinning. I mean, not *really* spinning—that would be weird because human heads are not designed to spin. In fact, a spinning head is probably fatal. . . .

Unless you're a zombie.

Oh man, zombie heads can spin. One time I whacked one with my hockey stick, and—

So maybe not technically spinning, but yeah—
we *are* confused. We just got whooped.
Whooped by a human!
A human who speaks the language of Ṛeżżőcħ!
A human who stole *my Louisville Slicer*!
I'm lost in a general sort of "feeling sorry for
myself" vibe—which is not a Jack Sullivan–type
feeling. I *never* feel sorry for myself. The worse
things get, the more gung-ho positive I am.
That's like my trademark!
Well, actually, the Louisville Slicer is my
trademark. And . . .
CRUD, SHE STOLE IT THE HUMAN STOLE
MY TRADEMARK!
I mean, what's Luke Skywalker without his
lightsaber? Just a farm boy with a whiny streak.
Or what's Katniss without her bow and arrow?
She's probably the first tribute to bite the big
one, that's what.

We're coming into Wakefield Town Square—
the place where me, my human buddies, and the
good-dude monsters live in awesome harmony.
Monster City!

And in Monster City I see worried monster
faces.

"Aww," I say. "That's nice. They're sad for me
'cause I don't have my bat."

"Jack, they have no idea you lost your bat,"
June says.

"Didn't lose," I say. "Stolen."

June sighs. "You know what I mean. . . ."

"Um, no—actually I *don't* know what you
mean. Retainers are lost. Phone chargers are
lost. This is *GRAND THEFT*!"

June groans. "OK, fine, Jack, whatever. Bottom
line: the reason the monsters are bummed is just
because now they're *extra* afraid of the snow."

June's right. I see it on their faces. Fear.

"No, no—the *winter* didn't hurt us. It was a bad human and a giant monster!" I shout.

I catch sight of Bardle. He's the first monster friend we got to know well. And he's eyeing me like he knows something is up. He beckons to us from the doorway of his home base, Joe's Pizza.

Moments later, we're inside, sitting in an old grease-stained booth. Bardle's across from me. . . .

Bardle.

Bardle pours me a cold grape soda, and I knock it back it one big swig. I was going to deliver a very serious, dramatic speech—but I start talking, my friends get excited, and it just comes out. . . .

Bardle's face freezes. "A human spoke that language? Are you certain?"

I nod.

"What did she say?" Bardle asks. "I must know the words!"

Quint is good with languages. He's been taking French, Spanish, and Bulgarian since like third grade. "I'm not certain I can pronounce it," he says. "It was something like . . . SOO ZUT CROOLER."

June knows Spanish, because her parents spoke it at home. Her attempt sounds like, "ZOUL SUT CRULLER."

"Guys, she didn't say *cruller*," I say. "Why would she say *cruller*? Crullers are delicious snake donuts and I don't think she was talking about snake donuts."

June sighs. "Jack, crullers aren't snake donuts. They're just long pastries that have—"

"NOPE! SNAKE DONUTS!" I say.

Dirk suddenly slams his fist on the table. His voice is a growl. "Guys, this is *serious*. Stop talking about snake donuts." He seems embarrassed to try, but then says, "Bardle, I heard something like—ahem— SUU ZOULT KRUELER."

Bardle's eyes narrow. Whatever Dirk said—he got it right. Bardle gently massages one of his long ear hairs. "This means . . . IT HAS BEGUN."

"Wait—*what's* begun?" June asks.

Suddenly a cold darkness seems to pass over the room. I shiver. The lights flicker. It's a coincidence, I'm sure—just ice on the generator—but it's eerie.

Bardle shakes his head. "I do not know what's begun. But for some reason, a human speaks the language of Ṛeżżőcħ. That human stole your blade. And with it, that human has begun *something.*"

Bardle suddenly stands. . . .

chapter five

That night, the strange human villain haunts my dreams, like the baddie in an '80s horror movie. . . .

I wake up shivering. Partly from the cold—
because yeah, IT IS FREEZING. My winter
sleeping outfit is someone's weird old Halloween
CHEWBACCA COSTUME. And Quint's
makeshift heater—a bunch of PlayStations
and Xboxes piled on top of one another—is not
working.

But mostly, it's a shiver of fear.

That was a *human* villain. A human villain
using MY WEAPON as part of a bad-dude plan.
We need to find that human and retrieve my
Louisville Slicer. And soon! Because if this
monster-riding human decides to attack, I'm
afraid we're unprepared. . . .

See, our *monster town* is now a *ghost town*.
The monsters are huddled up inside stores
and shops inside Wakefield Town Square, too
terrified of the snow to come out.

This *must* be fixed.

I brew some hot chocolate, and the smell
soon has my buddies waking. "Guys," I say.
"This villain lady knows stuff about R̩eżżőcħ.
So, if a fight goes down—and fights DO KIND
OF ALWAYS GO DOWN AROUND HERE—then
we need our monster buddies ready to rumble
alongside us. And they are *not* ready to rumble."

Moments later, we're outside having a—
LIGHT-HEARTED, JUST-HORSING-AROUND,
BUDDY SNOWBALL BATTLE!

"Isn't winter the best?!" I shout as I hurl a
snowball.

"Such a delight!" June says.

Monsters start watching. Some are huddled up

in blankets, peering through frosty windows. I think I even see one watching through a mailbox slot. I grin.

"Guys, play up the fun!" I whisper. "Everyone loves a good friendly snowball fight!"

That's when Quint appears on the deck of the tree house with an armful of snowball artillery. Our old-fashioned snowball battle turns awesomely post-apocalyptic and gadgetfied.

Dirk wields our old Tennis Blaster 2000—which is now the *Mobile Snow Sphere Slinger*—and things get intense. . . .

We're all giggling and laughing and freezing.

And it's working. A monster comes shambling out and joins the fun!

Unfortunately, that monster is Biggun. He scoops up a Biggun-sized snowball and—

FROSTY BIGGUN BLAST!

BAP

And that's the end of that. The Biggun Blast freezes us to the core. We spend the rest of the day in the tree house, huddled up near the video game systems, trying to get warm.

And the monsters are now *extra* freaked out. They've become afraid of snow in both *flake* form and *ball* form.

When we've finally finished thawing out, Dirk makes a suggestion: ice fishing.

"Fish for ice?" I ask. "Why would we *fish* for *ice*? Ice is everywhere! The whole world is basically a Super Mario snow level."

"No, dork," Dirk says. "You fish for fish *through* a hole in the ice. It's my favorite part about winter. C'mon. I know a spot."

We convince Skaelka and a few other monsters to join us. They agree—but only after I promise they'll get to eat GIANT HUNKS OF RAW FISH.

We're walking along a wooded trail, freezing our butts off, when I hear movement in the trees.

"Whoa, look!" Junes says. "Two little critters just went tumbling past!"

Skaelka halts. A strange snarl sound escapes her nostrils and her hands tighten around her ax. She suddenly means business.

"What's the alone one?" June asks.

"One not in the community," Skaelka says. "One that does not matter."

And the way Skaelka says it—it's clear the conversation is over. Skaelka is no big fan of the *alone one*.

At the lake, I learn something that's a bummer: ice fishing is the most boring thing on earth. You drill a hole in the ice and you just sit there! That's literally it! THE WHOLE THING! You can't even *talk* because apparently that "scares away the fish."

49

After the fifth hour of cold nothingness, I say, "If monsters don't get me first, I *will* die of boredom."

"Hey! No talking!" Dirk says. "Listen to nature. Hear the peace and quiet and—"

ICE TENTACLE BURST!

BE GONE, COLD ONE!

Oh, dear! Such horror!

Such slicing!

So . . . fishing was a big fat icy fail. The only thing we caught was a cold. And there's no way Quint with a runny nose is going to get *any creature* excited about winter.

I'm sitting in the tree house, bemoaning all this, when Quint says, "SNOWMEN!"

"Snow *creatures*!" June declares.

I keep my mouth shut—but I have thoughts on snowmen. One word: OVERRATED. It's one of those things that *sounds* awesome but is never as good as you think it's going to be. I always start off excited about building some massive amazing snowman, but then a few hours later—

It's OK. I guess. . . .

Lame, new kid!

HUR HUR HUR

But, we actually do pretty good! Dirk is, like, a master snow craftsman. He even gets out a tool kit and carves a totally beautiful ice sculpture. Dude is full of hidden talents.

It's going well—until the monsters get a load of our constructions—and then it goes *bad.* . . .

"What about ice skating?" June asks. "Ice skating is fun. And before you give me grief—I'm not talking *regular* ice skating. I'm talking *end-of-the-world-ice-skating.* Down the old highway that runs to the beach and boardwalk!"

Dirk's in, because he's a hockey master. June's in, because she's generally athletic, nimble, and above-average at everything. Quint's in because he doesn't like being left out of things.

It goes awry—of course.

It goes awry because this massive hibernating horror wakes up and goes *nuts. . . .*

I'm beat; totally out of ideas for turning our monster friends into winter-lovers. And even worse, we're no closer to figuring out what the deal is with the Villainess and what she did with my Louisville Slicer! She could be—I dunno—slow dancing with it right now!

Argh.

I need a long winter nap. So I head to our hammock, but when I get there, I see that June's beat me to it. And she looks even more bummed out than I feel.

Oh, real quick—our hammock is not a regular hammock. It's a monster winter hammock and it's kind of the best.

See, after the temperature dropped we discovered that one monster—Kylnn—constantly radiates heat. His whole body feels like some sort of living fireplace!

So I, being a napping *expert*, grabbed a hammock from the local Home Depot and strung it up. I suspended it from Kylnn's biggest back spikes. I'm pretty sure I have created the single most snuggly sleeping spot on planet Earth.

I sit down next to June. We lie there for a bit, just quietly looking up at a cloudy blue sky.

"You OK, buddy?" I finally ask.

June shrugs and pushes off from a spike, swinging us out. "It's just all this winter stuff. It reminds me of—y'know—*Christmas*. It's got me thinking about last year's Christmas. *Normal Christmas*."

June shoots me a look. Oh right. I forgot. She doesn't love the "monster-zombie-crossbow-filled adventure-scape" the same way I do.

June continues. "When we were getting ready to set out on our road trip for New York, I had this idea. I'm sure it was just a total pipe dream of a hope—but I thought we might get to New York. And find my family. And in time for Christmas. Then I could celebrate Christmas, for real. But I guess not. . . ."

I'm not sure what to say. See, I was an orphan, never had a real family. When the world went to the monsters, my foster family of the month fled. Here, with my buddies and our monster community, I finally feel like I *do* have a family. But for my human friends—it's the opposite.

Sometimes I forget that the gung-ho happiness that comes so easy to me is way harder for everyone else. And I *can't* keep forgetting that.

It's not right.

It's not being a good friend.

And being a post-apocalyptic monster-battling tornado of wannabe cool—that stuff's great, that stuff's important. But it's not even a *fraction* as important as being a solid buddy. And that's what June needs right now.

Then it hits me. Two birds, one stone!

I sit up and grab June by the shoulders. "June, I can't give you that classic family Christmas—but together we CAN have our own totally original joy-missile of a Christmas with *just* our best buddies in the world! We can make up our own new traditions! Like Christmas fireworks—aren't those the best?"

"Christmas fireworks aren't a thing, Jack."

"THEY ARE NOW!" I say. "Also, Christmas pie-eating contests! June, this is actually *amazing*. We have the chance to design our own awesome Christmas. Just as crazy, weird, and *whatever* as we want!"

June shifts in the hammock. She blows into her hands, thinking. "And you know what—since Christmas is the best . . ."

I smile and nod. "If there's one thing that can convince the monsters that winter is A-OK, it's Christmas!"

"Boom," June says. "Seal it with a fist bump."

We walk back to the tree house. At the ladder, June suddenly stops. She looks deep into my eyes. I'm wondering if this might be sort of a romantic moment or something, but instead . . .

"You've got your Louisville Slicer, and you love it!" June says. "I want to feel that sort of love for a monster-battling weapon."

It's true.

My love for the Louisville Slicer is a once-in-a-lifetime love. I could write a song about it.

And—June deserves that sort of love!

That will be my Christmas gift to her. One post-apocalyptic monster-battling tool TO RULE THEM ALL!

And you know what else?

I have lost my love.

No. Worse. My love was stolen from me! It has fallen into the hands of an enemy! And that enemy is up to *something*.

I'm not just waiting around. I need to *go and get it*. I need to find out WHO this villain is. Because only then will I get what *I* want for Christmas. . . .

chapter six

Quint wakes me up and I groan. "Dude, I was in the middle of a dream! I was in a big field and I was riding Rover and I was swinging the Louisville Slicer and it was warm and I had a cool mustache. Can you just let me go back to sleep?"

But Quint says, "I think I know how to find the Villainess."

"SAY WHAT?" I instantly leap to my feet.

Quint smiles and holds up the card that the Villainess dropped. I completely forgot about it! "It's a library card!" Quint says. "We can get her name at the library! And maybe her address!"

"And that'll lead us to her. And to the Louisville Slicer!" I say. "LET'S DO THIS."

I try to gather the squad—but they're busy. June is plotting how best to explain Christmas to the monsters. "I don't want it to be lousy like the fishing or the snowmen or ice skating," she explains. "I want to introduce them to Christmas so perfectly that they *have* to love it."

Meanwhile, Dirk is working on Big Mama. Who knows why he's bothering. We already know it can't make it all the way to New York until the snow passes. Maybe he's polishing it or putting on some cool spinning rims or something.

It's all good, though, 'cause now it'll be a . . . CLASSIC QUINT & JACK DUO ESCAPADE!

Quint has invented a way for us to get there. See, Rover does *not* like the snow. He's got sensitive paws or something.

So Quint reveals . . .

The winter HOVERBOARD!

It's super rad. But I don't know *why* these things are called hoverboards. There is ZERO HOVERING. I've seen *Back to the Future Part II* and I know that a hoverboard is supposed to legit *hover*. This is a rolling balance thing. But, regardless—it's pretty awesome. Only problem, despite Quint's winterizing modifications, it's still a little slippery. . . .

We arrive bruised and cold—and not eager to use hoverboards again.

The library is an old building that's awesome, but also creepy. It was built in, like, the 1800s. I don't know if you're good with dates and stuff like I am—but that's a long time ago.

I scan for danger. I see none. I hear none. But I'm a post-apocalyptic action hero, so I know that doesn't mean there *is* none.

"Steel yourself, Quint," I growl, as we roll toward the entrance. "Probably all manner of terror awaiting us."

BAM

All right, undead librarians, zombie old folks trying to figure out the internet, and monster-sized bookworms—prepare to meet our fists!

Or not. ...

We are greeted by zero undead librarians, no zombie old folks attempting to "surf the web," and no monster-sized bookworms, snakes, caterpillars, or Wormungulouses.

"The coast is clear," Quint says. "So I'm getting to work!"

He hops off his hoverboard and quickly goes behind the front desk. "I can't believe I'm getting a peek behind the library counter!" he says giddily. "It's a dream come true!"

This is the stuff that gets my buddy excited.

See, before I moved to Wakefield, Quint had zero friends. After I moved to Wakefield, he had one friend. (That friend was *me*, in case you were having trouble following the math.)

But during those years where Quint had zero friends—he spent his time at the library. Libraries are awesome like that. They should have that Statue of Liberty sign out front—y'know, give us your tired, your poor, your huddled masses yearning to read graphic novels. Libraries rule because everyone's welcome!

"Good news, friend!" Quint says as he yanks open a filing cabinet. "No computer needed—this library keeps physical records!"

He searches by library card ID number. In just moments—

"FOUND HER!"

BOOM. LOVE IT. Classic Quint and Jack Duo Escapade is off to a perfect start!

Quint steps around the desk, waving a folder. My heart pounds. "Inside that vanilla folder," I say, "is the name of our enemy."

"*Manila* folder," Quint says. "With an *m*. Why would a folder be vanilla?"

"Um, because it's like white-yellow-ish—the color of vanilla. Why would it be MANILA? That's not even a WORD."

"It is," Quint says with a sigh. "Trust me. But what you were saying is correct—inside this MANILA FOLDER is . . ."

The name. Of the villain. He opens it.

I read: EVIE SNARK.

I say the name, over and over, inside my head. *Evie Snark.* She is the villain. She is the human who speaks the language of Ŗeżżőcħ.

"OK, fight time," I say. "I'm ready to storm this villain's house and do a full-on battle attack fist-eating Louisville recovery raid!"

Quint frowns. "Alas, there is no address listed for this Evie Snark. But there still may be more to learn here! Look, her checkout history! She took out a LOT of books from a library section called Obscure Beliefs and Strange History. Come, friend!"

Obscure Beliefs and Strange History turns out to be the weirdest part of the library. It's in a back corner of the basement, and it is the absolute most dusty, most musty. It doesn't look like anyone's been here since the days of Nintendo 64—though I guess Evie Snark *must* have been here at some point.

Quint plops down, cross-legged, and plucks a book from the shelf. I see what's happening. He's going to sit here, going through book after book, page by page, for the next, oh, nineteen hours or so.

And that is nineteen hours that I do *not* want to be a part of. I want to fast-forward to the part where we get back my Louisville Slicer.

"Quint, buddy, enjoy the research. I hear the graphic novels calling my name."

"Mm-hmm, OK," Quint murmurs as I zip off.

But I don't make it to the graphic novels. I pass the DVD section, and that gives me a lightning bolt of an idea! I can help June! What better way to help show monsters the wonders of Christmas than with a Christmas movie marathon?

I jam a dozen of my favorite Christmas movies into my bag.

And then I smell it.

Not evil.

In fact, the very *opposite* of evil.

Reese's Peanut Butter Cups.

I whirl around: a vending machine! AKA a Happiness Dispenser. And it could not come at a better time—after our icy ride through the snow, I'm ravenous.

Two problems. One—I have no coins. Two—there's no electricity, so even if I had coins, they'd be useless. Normally, I could whip out the Louisville Slicer and go berserker mode on this thing. . . .

Yes! Yes! Come to me, sweet candy!

Not you, granola bar, you stay there.

Without my Louisville Slicer, I am—again—basically helpless. But I've got my trademark Jack Sullivan unattractive, gangly arms! I can reach up in there and totally, no problem, nab that Reese's!

In a flash, I'm down on my butt, sort of half turned over. "Oh yeah. Come to Jack, sweet chocolate. Come to daddy-o."

I've almost got it, and—

Crud. My arm is stuck. Pinched between metal and candy!

No problem—I'll just, uh—do a cool bone manipulation thing and yank my arm out, and—

Crud. Again.

A new smell. Have you ever smelled dog vomit? Imagine that, smothered in BBQ sauce.

I look up—and I gulp.

Some sort of monstrous, slurping, aboveground-like *octopus* is dragging itself toward me. . . .

"Hey, creepy aboveground octopus. Just FYI: my arm may be stuck, but I'm still *totally* a heroic hero and I'm totally in control and I *will* bust you up, SO STAY PUT!"

The thing keeps coming. But it's OK. I know 100 percent exactly how to handle this. . . .

I yank and pull but—ahh, fisticuffs!—I'm stuck elbow-deep! Argh. I need, like—I dunno—Mega Man's blaster! Or Wolverine's claws! Or Ash's chainsaw arm! Any wrist-attached weapon would be a big help here. Or MY FREAKING LOUISVILLE SLICER!

The wet beast slithers forward, and—
I GOT IT!

I mean, I don't "got it" in the sense that I
know what to *do*, but . . . I GOT THE REESE'S!

OK, I get that
you want to suck my
face off. But—could I
eat the Reese's first?

SNARL!

Is that a no?
How about if we
split it? It's the
extra-thick kind!

It's coming, I'm done for, and then—

BOOM!

A rolling library cart slams into the monster. There's a wet *SPLAT* and the monster is suddenly airborne, sailing across the library! Books fly. Pages flap. Quint grins down at me from atop the cart.

"Hello, friend," he says. "Looks like you needed a bit of rescuing."

The vending machine falls. It takes me with it, flipping me over, but—

I pop out! Arm free! We hop on the cart, roll out the door, and speed away across the ice. . . .

"How'd the reading go?" I ask.

"Didn't get much done. I had to bring the books with me so I can keep going through them. I heard your cowardly cry."

Cowardly cry! *Me?*

"However!" Quint exclaims. "More important is *this*! I discovered that the Villainess—Evie Snark—stopped going to the library after she owed *NINE HUNDRED DOLLARS* in overdue library fees."

"Are you kidding me?"

Quint grins. "And it was all for one book. . . ."

Getting back is not easy. We eventually abandon
the library cart when it gets stuck in the snow,

but that means a *long* walk. Near the outskirts of town, I spot something in the distance. A massive structure, rising up from the snow.

"What is that?" I ask Quint.

Quint glances around, and then he sees what I see. He begins muttering, "Oh no. Oh no, oh no, oh no."

"What is it, buddy? Some bad evil?"

"Not quite," Quint says. "It's—oh, it's so embarrassing. . . ."

He rummages through his wallet and pulls out a newspaper clipping. "That's the ABC Block Smasher Cinema. And I got it shut down. . . ."

"Wait—you *shut down a movie theater*?"

Quint nods. "I had a problem: my allowance was only enough money for the ticket—no snacks! And you *know* I can't enjoy the cinema without delicious treats! So, I began smuggling in candy bars and whatnot. But one day I came home *covered* in chocolate Goobers goo. My mom *knew* I only had enough money for the ticket, so she called the theater!"

"She ratted?!" I gasp.

"The next time I went to see a movie, there was a picture of me at the ticket booth! A big note said KEEP AN EYE ON THIS BOY."

"But revenge was mine!" Quint says. "I was watching the latest Marvel blockbuster when I discovered a loose floor panel beneath my seat. Eureka! I smuggled in snacks enough to last an entire summer of blockbusters—and I *hid them in the floor*!

"After that, every time I went to the movies I'd go to my spot, flip it open, and eat like a king! It went fine—until one day when *THE CANDY WAS GONE*!"

"Someone found your snack stash?!" I exclaim.

"Not someone," Quint says. "A RAT! The fattest rat you ever saw! It leapt out at me. It had eaten approximately nineteen pounds of sweet treats!"

I start laughing. And then I finish unfolding the newspaper clipping. . . .

LOCAL BOY OVERPOWERED BY TINY RODENT

by Leila Sales, Media Expert

Quint shakes his head. "The movie theater company called in exterminators—but it was too late. The rats had become addicted to sweets, gotten super mean, made a bunch of mean rat babies, and the movie theater was one big mean rat playground."

"DUDE!" I exclaim. "HOW MUCH CANDY DID YOU HIDE?"

"A lot," Quint says with a sigh. "They had just reopened the theater for the summer, Jack. Right before the Monster Apocalypse. Movies were playing! But word on the street was there were *still* rats scurrying around. . . ."

We continue our long trek back home. "I can't believe you shut down an entire movie theater, buddy."

Quint shrugs. "It was not my proudest moment."

chapter seven

So it's called Christmas—and it's my favorite thing ever.

Coming into town, it's clear that June has basically declared herself the *mayor* of Christmas. Which—let's be honest—is a pretty rad title. But it also means we can't mess up because if Christmas is lousy, who's everyone gonna blame? The Mayor of Christmas, that's who.

The monsters ask a few questions—and I realize, they *are* fair questions. . . .

OK, so they're confused by stockings and
the trees. But we have an ace up our sleeve. A
grand salami we can pull from our back pocket.
Something *guaranteed* to get everyone wet-your-
pants excited.

I race up to join June in the tree house. I stare
at the monster crowd below, and I exclaim,
"GIFTS! PRESENTS!"

"Gurfts?" a monster asks.

"Prezeezes?" another says.

"Hold up," June says. "Do you guys *not* know
what gifts are? Presents?"

Apparently, the entire *concept* of gift giving is totally foreign to the monsters! It simply does not exist in their dimension. Just like *they* have stuff that doesn't exist in *our* dimension, that *we* think is weird. For example . . .

A cheerful monster named Murgy chirps up. "You give an item to another being? To make them feel good? Gifts sound simply joyous!"

With that, the monsters are *in*. And now, we all must put together . . .

*THE ULTIMATE END-OF-THE-WORLD
CHRISTMAS!*

First up: the TREE. We need a *whopper*. No
dinky, half-dead Charlie Brown thing here. I
want a full-on Rockefeller Center deal! I mean,
we can grab any tree we want from anywhere!
No trekking out to the tree stand and lamely just
pointing at one. No, we do it post-apocalyptic
style. . . .

Biggun.

Zombie Mr. Schmeed. One
time he freaked out at Quint
and me for cutting through
his backyard, so now his tree
is OURS!

RIP!

Next: decorating this bad boy.

The key to killer Christmas tree decorating is good ornaments. Sadly, we have *zero* ornaments.

But our neighbors do! We raid nearby houses, digging through garages and basements. I find ornaments and lights and tinsel—and also a few gnarly surprises. . . .

Problem: Our tree's height makes decorating difficult. But it's all good. Quint takes a break from studying Evie Snark's reading list to trick out an old leaf blower, turning it into the . . .

BULB BLASTER! It can practically send ornaments into orbit!

Simply drop the decoration into the blower, and then—

Bare spot, right there!

Got it!

PWOOF!

At night, we snack on food from my post-apocalyptic advent calendar. Advent calendars are a good idea—and opening up the little flappy window is fun—but it always bugged me how the candy inside was so small and dinkified! And then grown-ups would try to pass off that minuscule candy morsel like it's a legit dessert.

So I have UPDATED the advent calendar.
Please meet: JACK SULLIVAN'S CHRISTMAS
COUNTDOWN OF COPIOUS CANDY. . . .

And maybe *most* important . . .
I KNOW WHAT TO GET JUNE FOR CHRISTMAS!
The gift idea came to me after I escaped that
arm-eating vending machine and the library
squid-beast. I'm slightly nervous about this gift,
because it's homemade. But I'm pretty sure June
will like it.

And I promise: It will *not* be lousy. Homemade
gifts get a bad rap, which is fair, because they're
not always the best.

I mean, a handmade knickknack is totally sweet and heartfelt—but, I promise, your dad would rather have a Ferrari than a crummy pencil holder.

But my gift to June will *not* be crummy and it will *not* hold pencils! Quint and Dirk are helping me, and it's going to be *ridiculous*. . . .

June's sound system—which is THE BOMB—blasts Christmas tunes all day, every day. And I project movies onto the side of Joe's Pizza, so we can all enjoy *Elf* together.

One afternoon, Dirk and June and I are playing Monopoly. June's singing along to music. And Dirk's nodding and humming.

I smile.

I smile because despite the crazy weirdness of this monster world—we're putting together the greatest Christmas I've ever been a part of. . . .

That's when Quint comes clambering up into the tree house. And he tells us.

He tells us something that I suspect, I feel, will change *everything*. A location. A place.

It's like finding the map to Luke Skywalker. If Luke Skywalker was a creepy weirdo who stole kids' baseball bats.

"I know where the Villainess resides," Quint announces proudly. "I found her address in the phone book. And that means we may know the location of the Louisville Slicer. . . ."

"YES!" I try to do one of those off-the-floor ninja flip-kick things. I fail. I definitely maybe twist my ankle, almost sprain my back. But no worries, because . . .

chapter eight

Evie Snark lives across town, in Wakefield's historic district—near the shore and the old port. And we're stuck hoofing it. The combination of Rover's sensitive footsies and out-of-commission Big Mama means we're getting some serious cardio. . . .

"Look," June says. Ahead of us is a steep, winding brick road lined with ancient-looking houses.

Quint consults his map. "We're close."

It's only another ten minutes of hiking before we've found the Villainess's home. . . .

The numbers on Evie Snark's mailbox hang crooked from rusty screws. The house is gray and the paint is chipped. The curtains have turned yellow. Bits of tall, never-mowed grass poke through the high snow. I don't recognize *this* house—but I recognize the general idea. . . .

See, *every* town I've ever lived in has one house like this; a house that looks like it's celebrating Halloween year-round. Maybe every town *everywhere* has this house. That house that when you're walking the dog, you cross the street so you don't get infected by the heebie-jeebies.

I know it's just a trick in my brain—but I can almost *smell* the Louisville Slicer inside the house. The mix of baseball diamond wood and splattered monster guts and palm sweat.

It's here, in Evie Snark's house.

Evie Snark: the Villainess who speaks the language of Ŗeżżőcħ.

Dirk finds a weak spot in the fence. He grabs it, gloves wrapping tight around the metal, and bends one bar. We squeeze through, then carefully creep up the hill. We are basically masters of stealth. Until—

KRAK!

The ice at my feet is splitting. My snow sneaker plunges through, and an instant later, we're all up to our waists in absolute freezing-ness.

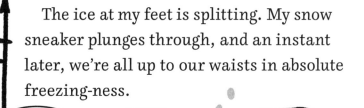

Oh, dear. The Villainess who speaks the language of Reżżöch has a private pond!

I can't take these cruddy clothes anymore! Too cold!

I'm tough. But not tougher than frostbite.

"What do you want to do? Go back?!" I exclaim, as I pull myself out of the cold water, then point to the house. "We're close!"

"*Close to freezing!*" June says.

Quint quickly replies, "June, you might be *cold*, but your body temperature is far from the ninety-five degrees that indicates freezing and hypothermia."

June's lip curls. "Quint. We're friends. But I *will* bury you in a pile of snow."

"We'll get dry inside," I say. I spot a window that is a few inches open. The dingy yellow curtains flap in the arctic breeze. I listen carefully. I'm hoping my Spidey-sense will kick in and tell me whether anyone's home.

It does not.

Sadly, loving Spider-Man does not actually *give* you Spidey-sense.

I must breach this creepy fortress. . . .

The window's small—but I've fit through tighter spots while playing flashlight tag. I know I should be cautious, but now that we're close—I WANT MY BLADE.

"Dirk, boost me!" I whisper. In a flash, my
sneaker is in his hand, and I'm up into the
window. I get halfway through—then I'm totally
jam-stuck.

"I've been waiting so long to kick your rear
end," June says. I can almost *hear* her grinning.

WOMP! June's boot meets my butt and I'm
propelled through the window. Loud enough to
alert anyone who's home.

Slowly, I stand.

What I see is so shocking that I just about
swallow my tongue. . . .

chapter nine

"Guys," I say. "You're *not going to believe this!*"

This joint isn't creepy—it's a geek's dream come true! It's *my* dream come true. It's dusty and it's cramped and it's filled to the brim with *geek stuff.*

I spot cases crammed with comic and cinematic collectibles! The actual outfit that Batman wore in the movie from 1989! A Ghostbusters marshmallow man model!

Even the Villainess's *bathroom* is loaded with reproduction movie cannons and blasters, and the walls are covered with swords, axes, and blades. And also toilet paper 'cause, y'know, she is a human. . . .

This is a *lifetime's* worth of MAJOR collecting. It's a museum. Her own, personal museum.

Quint peeks his head in the window. "Is it safe?" he asks.

"I'm not sure if it's safe," I say, "but I am sure it's awesome. Get in here, gang!"

A moment later . . .

There's no sign of the Villainess, Evie Snark.
And honestly, I'm so *totally* overwhelmed by how
cool this is that, for a moment, I forget about
her. We all do. My buddies are instantly yanking
things off walls and shelves.

"Dudes," I say, "we've stumbled upon an oasis of nerd awesomeness."

"It's the holy grail of geekiness," Quint says, in the most serious voice I've ever heard.

I'm trembling—partly from how excited I am by this geek collection, and partly from the ice water in my underwear. But those icy undies make me realize—we don't need to be freezing our butts off, looking like bootleg monster slayers, as we stomp around Wakefield. Now we can dress for the winter like *heroes*.

"Guys, look around!" I say. "Do you realize what we can do with this stuff? Forget our lame old sweaters and ziplock not-quite-waterproof socks. We can build our own winter action outfits!"

"Huh?" Dirk grunts.

"We're *basically* post-apocalyptic action heroes!" I go on. "So we need to dress like it! We need to UPGRADE!"

"A major costume change is a very big deal," Quint says.

"A very big *awesome* deal!" I say. "You know how whenever a new Batman movie or a new X-Men movie comes out and *Entertainment Weekly* has, like, nineteen pages about the new costumes? That'll be us! Like: Jack, June, Quint, Dirk—*check out what these heroic awesome people are wearing this season!*"

I stop to picture my dream winter action costume. I glance at Quint—and I *know* we're both thinking the same thing. . . .

"I dig it," June says.

And with that we get to work. . . .

I'm stepping into a pair of Batman pants when I stumble into a glass display case. Inside is a replica *Assassin's Creed* wrist-dagger gizmo—and I realize something *else*.

This is TOTALLY the place where I can put June's Christmas gift over the top! Her gift is almost complete—but now I can make it *perfect*.

Because any movie or gaming or comic book weapon used for fighting bad dudes *also* works for battling giant monsters.

I can almost picture June now. . . .

My June-as-battle-mage thoughts are interrupted by Dirk and Quint. They've found replica Harry Potter wands and are having a wizard's duel, which turns into a game of Muggle baseball when Quint hurls a Golden Snitch at Dirk.

"PERFECTO!" June suddenly exclaims. "The final piece of my costume."

June is racing toward a pair of General Leia boots. I'm falling behind in winter action outfit creating!

I hurry up, trying on a Venom costume, Black Widow boots, creepy clown coat, and I even throw a superhero shield over my back.

My buddies tuck their inflatable donut rafts beneath their new gear and we are ready! We can battle in snow! Ice water is no threat! I could curl up for a nap on Starkiller Base and stay toasty! Because we have . . .

- WINTER ACTION GETUPS! -

Northern king coat

Judge Dredd shoulder pads

Super Mario gloves

Jedi robes

Galactic general and princess boots

99

That's when I notice the door. Curiosity grabs me. I walk over, pull it open—and I see a room full of something strange.

Thousands upon thousands of action figures.

"Whoa . . ." I whisper. They are arranged on the floor like some sort of action-figure army. Transformers, Lego figures, Ninja Turtles, DC Funkos—a bit of *everything*.

But something about these figures is *not right*.

I peer closer—and I realize. The figures have all been altered. Modified. Customized.

"*Zombified* . . ." a voice says.

I turn. It's Quint. He's examining one of the figures. Dirk and June follow him.

"She's zombified them," Quint says. "Custom paints and dyes. Arms yanked off. Legs severed at their joints. Some appear to have been *melted*."

I grab a handful of figures—and I see it's true. She has taken thousands upon thousands of collectible figures—and made each one appear *undead*.

Wolverine, hands gone.

Batman, with a distorted face.

Teen Titans, skin gray and plastic insides exposed.

It's like stumbling upon some monstrous
animal's secret lair, full of bones.

"Jack," June whispers. "Look there. Mounted
above the fireplace."

I see it. The one thing in the room that *isn't* a
fake zombie figure. . . .

The Louisville Slicer.

I shove the zombified figures that I'm holding into my jacket pocket. Standing on my tippy-toes, I reach for the Louisville Slicer. . . .

While I'm reaching, I see Quint. Our dorky, geeky eyeballs connect.

"Jack, don't!" Quint whispers.

Finger-snap quick, we're on the same page: we need to get *out of this joint*. Because it's suddenly *clear*. In my mind, everything is lighting up—like a video game that flashes and highlights items that you can use.

This is a trap.

But even as I realize it, my fingers are wrapping around the Louisville Slicer. It's like my brain is quicker than my body. No wonder I'm so lousy at basketball. But I'm also medium-good at video games? That's hand-eye coordination, too, right? Shouldn't I be equally good at ALL the hand-eye things?

I tug at the Louisville Slicer, and—

CLICK!

The bat moves. Just slightly.

Then the sounds begin: like a ball rolling, gears turning, or weights dropping. It's like stealing the idol in *Raiders of the Lost Ark*.

"The Louisville Slicer," Quint says. "It was connected to . . . I don't know—something!"

"What did you do?" Dirk whispers.

"Something dumb," I reply.

I glance back at my friends. They're huddled together in the center of the room. And a perfect square at their feet is swinging open . . .

WHOOSH!

Their eyes go wide and their mouths go wider. It's a trapdoor. I race toward them, diving, sliding, but they're already falling. And I'm falling too. . . .

Into darkness. . . .

chapter ten

Falling.

Then a painful *SNAP* feeling around my ankles—like how I imagine a crocodile might chomp. Then a weightless, stomach-flipping swinging.

"Why?" June asks. "And where are we?"

I twist my body to look up. I see the hole that we just fell through, now about eight feet above us. Not much light shines down. But I can see the four long ropes that currently hold us. And what looks like a gigantic pirate wheel or something, mounted on the ceiling.

This room is strangely deep. Not like a regular basement.

"Old smugglers' home," Dirk says. "We're near the docks. They had tunnels that led all over town."

"My flashlight!" Quint says. Of course he has his flashlight with him. Because who leaves their house without a flashlight? It better not be another zombie ball we see. . . .

He fishes into his pocket, pulls out the lamp, and flicks it on. A beam of light slices straight up through the darkness.

"It's a gear," Dirk says. "It controls the ropes."

My nose tickles. A smell is wafting up from below. I know that smell. I don't want to look—but I have to. I reach out, grab Quint's flashlight, and he directs the light down.

"Zombies . . ." June says softly.

If Evie Snark were a regular villain who wanted to do us in, she'd just, y'know—DO US IN. But she seems to be taking her moves straight from the Indiana Jones or James Bond playbook.

No question: She's impressive. We're dealing with some sort of queen geek. . . .

Suddenly, a rumbling. "I've got a bad feeling about this," I murmur.

GRRRMMMM...

"It's the gear above us!" June says. "It's turning!"

Quint gasps. "And as it's turning, we're being lowered!"

There's a short moment where no one says a word—and then all of us are talking over one another. The general idea is: OH NO THIS IS BAD WE HAVE TO STOP THIS NOW.

Quint's flashlight flashes across the zombie faces below. Oh, great—illuminated terror, just what we need. They began snarling, snapping, and—worst of all—reaching upward, with sick, shriveled hands.

"There are five zombies down there!" Quint exclaims.

"There are going to be nine zombies down there if we don't stop this!" June says.

I paw at the rope. Useless. I reach for the wall. Too far. "HOW DO WE STOP IT?"

"Newton's cradle!" Quint exclaims. "Individually, we can't reach the walls—but by transmitting our force through one another, we might—"

"Yeah, yeah, sure!" I say, cutting off Quint. "Whatever it is, let's try it!"

Quint pushes off my shoulder and swings back into me. I slam into June and she plows into Dirk. Then it's back the other way—the force carries through us, and Dirk swings out and out—

"GOT THE WALL!" Dirk exclaims. He grips the wall. His feet kick. But then—

CRASH! He loses his grip and comes flying back. We all bounce around—then sag.

"That did not work. . . ." I mutter.

Lower and lower we go.

The long, gnarled arms of the zombies reach and reach. Closer and closer . . . It feels like all is lost.

"Jack," Quint says, sounding suspicious. "What is inside your instant-inflate donut raft? It's supposed to be empty! For inflating!"

I sigh. "Well, if these are gonna be my last words to you, bud, I guess I should probably tell you the truth. I ignored your inflatable donut raft advice. I filled mine with food. It's a food tube."

Quint glares.

"I don't need a human airbag around my butt, OK?" I say. "It's not helpful! But food is helpful. Who knows what sort of awful winter showdown trap we could end up in! We need food to survive if we end up trapped inside some freezing building for days, surrounded by zombies!"

I'm watching the zombies get closer and closer—but Quint still wants to talk about airbags!

"What sort of food is it?" Quint asks.

"Um. Gum . . ." I say.

June erupts. "GUM?! Gum's not even food! If you're stuck somewhere for days and need to survive, the WORST FOOD to bring is gum."

"I was craving Big League Chew!" I defend myself. "Also, when you're starving to death, gum is the best food because it lasts longer."

"Gum's not food!" Dirk roars.

"Gum is food! It goes in the mouth, it's food! And the chewing tricks your mind into thinking you're eating! It's science!"

"THAT'S NOT SCIENCE!" Quint roars. "GUM IS—"

"Just what we need!" June suddenly exclaims.

We all cock our heads toward her. The zombie howls echo. There's not much time.

"Listen!" she says. "The big gear up there. If we could stop it from turning . . .

"Then we would stop descending!" Quint says.

"We need to get gum in it!" June cries.

"And I know how to do it!" I say, reaching out. I yank Quint's bulb blaster from his back.

In a flash, my buddies have torn my raft open and we are jamming massive wads of bubble gum into our mouths. The sweet smell almost overpowers the revolting, undead stench. . . .

I glance down at the zombies. We're close—and getting closer.

I yank a baseball-sized wad of gum from my mouth and jam it into the blaster. "In, in!" I say, and Quint shoves his in. Dirk's is massive: It's the Dirk-wad.

June pulls the sticky gum ball from her mouth, but at that moment, the tallest of the zombies paws at my hand.

"Ahh!" I exclaim. "He's got me!"

In a flash, June puts her gum to good use—

No time. We have only three shots at this. . . .

I aim and squeeze the blaster handle. . . .

FWOOP! A bubble-gum ball splatters against the ceiling, high above us.

I aim again . . . and miss again.

The final bubble-gum ball. Dirk's. The softball-sized goo-wad. I fire, and—

SPLAT! The Dirk-wad hits the giant gear! As the wheel turns, I see the sticky strands stretching, straining to hold it in place.

A jolt. Everything shudders. "We're slowing down! We're stopping!" Quint says.

I exhale a huge sigh of relief right into a zombie's face. "So what now?" I wonder. "We just hang here like worms on a hook?"

"If we get out of this, I'm never going fishing again," Dirk says. "I swear. I promise."

I crane my neck. There's a door behind the zombies. It must lead to those tunnels that Dirk was talking about. And from beyond that door, I hear footsteps. Evie . . .

We stopped her zombie trap just in time—but that won't get us back the Louisville Slicer. Like Bardle said, that's what matters. Being reunited with the blade. Stopping whatever "has begun."

I turn my head to avoid a swiping zombie hand, and I whisper to my friends, "We need the Villainess to think her plan worked. We need her to think we were bit!"

They nod. And then—

I shout! Just really letting loose, right in those blasted zombie faces, and my friends follow my lead. . . .

A long, long moment passes. I smell zombie breath. Sort of. They don't actually breathe—but a foul toxic odor leaks from their lungs.

And then the door opens. A rectangle of light comes in. I see Evie's wide shoulders and her long cloak, silhouetted in the doorway.

She has no real weapon with her, only a sort of dog-catcher's lasso. She must use it to snag and capture zombies. Zombies aren't dogs!

Her voice is light and singsongy. "Soon I'll have four new little zombies to choose from. . . ."

She pulls a crank on the wall, and—
YANK!

The zombies are jerked against the wall, strapped into it. A smart design, really—Evie can walk through without getting bit.

But it also means that we could escape without getting bit. We just have to get past her. . . .

We continue hanging, not moving, playing like we're bait. But the moment she reaches for me . . .

"EAT GUM!" I hurl a handful of dry, shredded gum into her face.

Evie staggers back. I reach up and release myself. June, Dirk, and Quint follow my lead. Our feet hit the ground. Evie snarls and swings her lasso—and then I notice something.

A satchel hangs over Evie's shoulder. It's covered in geeky buttons and pins and patches. The flap is open and I see inside. It's the book *Interdimensional Terrors: A History of the Cabal of the Cosmic.* The one that Evie owes nine hundred dollars in overdue fines on.

I exclaim, "Quint, the book!"

Evie looks down—and her eyes pop wide in terror. She swings the lasso again, but I duck underneath. Her lasso rakes the superhero shield on my back. I pluck the book from her bag and spin away from her next lasso swipe.

"Good job, Jack!" Quint says.

"Come on!" June shouts, tugging my jacket. Dirk yanks open the door, and we rush past Evie, into a dark, dank basement tunnel.

"But the Louisville Slicer! It's upstairs!" I cry out.

"Escape is this way!" June says.

Two metal doors loom at the end of the old smugglers' tunnel. Dirk steamrolls ahead, barrels into them, and they burst open.

Far behind us, Evie cries out in anger. . . .

chapter eleven

The ice-cold air stings my lungs. The snowflakes are thick and heavy, but not thick and heavy enough to hide us from the monster. . . .

"We're not out of this yet!" I cry.

Meathook is lumbering toward us. A hateful roar comes from the bottom of his belly.

"We can escape down the hill!" June says. Just beyond the monster, the yard slopes down, leading to the steeper, hillier street beyond.

"Wait—what?" I exclaim. My buddies are already reaching down and pulling their rip cords. . . .

POOF!

POOF! POOF!

The inner tubes inflate. "Guys! No inner tube here, remember? I'm a no-inner-tube guy! I'm a gum guy!"

But they don't hear me.

One second, June, Dirk, and Quint are sprinting ahead—next, they're on their tubes, flying down the hill.

The ground quakes.

A rumble shakes the earth and makes my soul squeak in terror.

I turn just in time to see Meathook's big fist flashing in the air.

"Whoa!" I cry out as I try to avoid the blow.

But I'm too slow. I'm half-turned, trying to duck, when the massive hammerfist connects with my back.

There's a deafening—

BOING!

For a second, I think I'm done for. But then I realize—no! This was actually perfect! Meathook's fist struck the shield! I cushioned the blow! My terrible dodge caused him to hit me at such an angle that I'm now sailing through the air!

When I land, the shield acts *exactly* like a sled! Unfortunately, I'm *upside down on that sled*. The hill is rushing up, rocket-fast. Snow in my eyes. Wind snaps and howls in my ears.

I have *zero control* over this thing. I bang into a mailbox, and magazines dump on my head. I spin out into the street. I'd better not barf—I've got a superhero's shield, and superheroes don't barf.

I'm quickly catching up with my buddies ahead. Houses whir by. I catch a glimpse of Meathook's one huge hand. He's right behind us. I bang into a car, and the spinning stops, but I'm still zipping backward. I have a perfect view of Meathook, stomping fast, closing in!

"Where?" I cry. "I'm backward! Give me a heads-up so that I don't plow right—!"

SLAM!

There's the snowbank. I'm tossed into flight, and Meathook stumbles.

MEATHOOK DOWN!

The shield lands hard on the street. It's all black ice. I'm about to flip, but then—

"GOTCHA, DUDE!" June shouts.

I look down—June has me by my wrist. I lunge and grab Quint's hand. Quint swings then clings to Dirk. "Human action geek chain!" I exclaim. "I love it!"

I close my eyes as a snowbank swings up. We ride it, and then turn down another long hill.

That's when I hear it.

A monstrous howl that certainly belongs to some new, huge, horrific, *terrifying* beast.

"Oh man, I don't need this right now!" I grumble. I swear, the end of the world—it's like, "Yo, congrats, you escape one monster, but now there's another one around the corner!"

I see the monster's mouth first. And I realize it's *all mouth*. A gaping fang gateway . . .

Abominable Snow MOUTH!

"We're heading right for that thing!" I cry out.

"Friends!" Quint cries. "Pull nozzles and deflate inner tubes!"

I hear a series of *POPs* as they yank the plugs from their inner tubes. Then the loud *WHOOSH* of air escaping.

"Guys!" I cry. "Stop doing cool inner tube moves that I can't be a part of!"

The world is rushing up at ludicrous speed. But the shield is *attached* to my back—I can't just undo it! I want off this ride.

A bump spins me, and I see my buddies slowing to safe stops—sliding into big, cushy snowbanks. June cups her hands over her mouth and shouts, "JACK! STOP! YOU'RE GOING INTO THE MONSTER'S MOUTH!"

Yes, June, I am aware . . .

The monster's roar snaps my head forward. I'm screaming toward the Snow Mouth. I need to stop this thing. . . .

I lift my legs and then *jam* my heels into the street. I watch ice and snow erupt! My new boot heels are being worn away to nothing!

And as I slow, I'm able to reach around and unhook the shield.

"That's better . . ." I say.

I can smell the monster's mouth. I see fangs and a massive gullet, deep and dark and waiting. . . .

I jam my heels deeper into the snow, slowing and slowing, enough that I can finally dive off!

The shield slices out from beneath me, and—

chapter twelve

Home.

It takes hours, but we get there. And then we fall into that deep, black, dreamless sleep where it's like you could sleep forever.

What finally wakes me is the sound of Quint thinking. Thinking shouldn't even *be* a sound— but with Quint, it is. He's *hmm*ing and *ahh*ing.

He must sense that I'm awake, because he suddenly exclaims, "Jack! Come look at the book we nabbed from Evie!"

Yesterday's weirdness comes flooding back.

I'm freaked out by what happened—and I'm not the only one.

June and Dirk are sitting up, waking, and I see the worried looks on their faces. Did you ever have a sleepover where, like, someone revealed some crazy secret? Or you did something you shouldn't have? And the next morning you look at your friends in the cold light of day and you're all thinking, *Whoa. Last night was weird.*

That's what this is. . . .

Before I can process that, a monster calls
from outside, "Up and at the lives, humans! It
is the eve of your tree-chopping and gift-giving
jubilee!"

I sigh. Christmas Eve. I'm not sure we should
be focusing on that. Celebrating a holiday seems
nuts right now. I mean—priorities! There's
currently a bad dude on the loose who makes

a habit of keeping zombies trapped in her basement!

But I catch June eyeing me and shaking her head. "Jack," she says, "you promised a kick-butt Christmas. I'm not letting that crazy lunatic mess up our special non-family holiday."

I nod. "OK, June—a promise is a promise."

"I'm taking this book straight to Bardle—there is much to learn!" Quint says. "Call me when it's time for new traditions!"

Moments later, we're dressed, and June is dragging Dirk and me into the Town Square. "Christmas Eve, Christmas Eve, Christmas Eve!" she sings happily.

The monsters compliment our new winter action costumes. They now think costume changing is a part of Christmas Eve and they're bummed they don't have their own new getups.

Despite my Evie anxiety—I'm immediately sucked into festivity fun!

June, the mayor of Christmas, leads this jamboree. She hurls us headlong into the BEST CHRISTMAS EVER. We eat cookies and watch movies, and Skaelka even wears an ugly sweater.

Dirk says he's saving his tradition for last.
Fine by me, 'cause it'll probably leave us with
bruises.

Most important—I manage to sneak away and find a few moments to *complete June's gift*! I use some items from Evie's house to make it next-level awesome.

I'm lousy at wrapping stuff—so I get help. My helper is not super pleased. . . .

Keep your eyes shut. . . .

I cannot believe you're making me wrap my own present!

Of course, I still don't have *my* gift: the Louisville Slicer, returned. We're T-minus, like, six hours until Christmas—not looking good. . . .

And that's what I'm thinking about when Quint calls us into Joe's Pizza.

There's something in his voice that makes me nervous. Like this Christmas Eve—it might not be anything like we hoped. . . .

chapter thirteen

WHEN WE MET, JACK, I TOLD YOU OF Ŗeżżőch THE ANCIENT, A FORCE OF EVIL FROM OUR DIMENSION.

But this book from Evie makes clear—the legend of Ŗeżżőch existed here on Earth, too! **Not** just in the monster dimension! The book calls Ŗeżżőch one of the *Cosmic Terrors* from the *Cosmic Beyond*....

Bardle says, "Ŗeżżőch is the greatest of the Cosmic Terrors. But there are others—creatures nearly as powerful and dangerous as him."

"Is everyone who comes from your dimension a Cosmic Terror?" I ask. "Are you?"

Bardle shakes his head. He looks offended that I would even suggest such a thing. "The Cosmic Terrors are pure evil. And they are not just from *our* dimension—they are from *all* dimensions and, at the same time, from *no* dimensions. Immortal, endless—the Cosmic Terrors live in the space between space."

"According to this book," Quint says, "some people on Earth worshiped them thousands of years ago! They claimed to have once made contact with one of the Cosmic Terrors. Look . . ."

Quint flips the pages of the book until he comes to a large drawing.

I gasp. "A portal. We've seen something like that before. With Thrull!"

Quint nods. "Right. Apparently, these worshipers had some success. They called themselves the Cabal of the Cosmic."

"Cabal?" I ask. "What's that?"

"It means, like, group," June says. "A tight group."

"A clique . . ." I growl. "I hate cliques."

"What about Blarg?" Dirk asks "And the King Wretch?"

"Yeah," I say. "They have that evil stench that makes me *know* they aren't like the other good-guy monsters. And Thrull had it, too! Are *they* Cosmic Terrors?"

Bardle says, "They are Servants of the Cosmic Terrors. Any creature can be a Servant—they need not be from a specific dimension. They must only commit their lives to aiding Ŗeżżőcħ in his quest to take over worlds. And the foulest of the brutish beasts—the Dozers, the Winged Wretches—they are Soldiers of the Cosmic Terrors."

Quint looks at me. "Are you confused, Jack?"

I nod. "Little bit."

"Me too," Dirk says.

June holds up her hand. "Hang on. I think I got it. It's kinda like school. . . ."

You got the principal up top—then the vice principal, and then the teachers. And they're all ruling over us, the kids. Rezzöch's like the principal.

He's got a bunch of vice principals, and those are the rest of the Cosmic Terrors. And the teachers, those are like the Cosmic Servants—

Blarg, Thrull, the King Wretch. The Winged Wretches and Dozers are like teachers' helpers. And we're . . . well, we're still the kids, I guess.

E UNKNOWN
REZZÖCH!!
OTHERS?
BLARG
KING WRETCH
THRULL
MYSTERY GIRL
YUCKY VINES
DOZERS
WRETCHES

I'm starting to get it. And I don't like it. "So Evie—she's a loony tune who decided to be a Cosmic Servant, too, huh? Well—big-question time—WHAT DOES SHE WANT?"

"Based on her notes in the margins of this book, she intends to bring a specific Cosmic Terror to Earth," Bardle answers. "The book speaks of him as Ghazt the General."

Quint shakes his head sorrowfully. "What kind of a villain *writes* in a *library* book?!"

"Ghazt the General . . ." Dirk says softly. "Sounds bad."

"Well . . . HOW is she going to bring this Ghazt terror here?" I exclaim. "If we know her plan, maybe we can stop her!"

Bardle taps a page. "According to the symbology here, she is following a specific, ancient, three-step ritual. Step one of three: 'Recover an Artifact that has destroyed a Servant to the Cosmic Terrors.'"

I look down, thinking hard. My eyes trace the cracked, splintered tile floor. I remember what Evie said, when we first encountered her. *"It has begun."*

I lift my head. I see my friends. It hits all of us. A horrible moment of revelation and absolute terror. . . .

"Wait up!" I say. "How would Evie even *know* the Slicer slayed Blarg?"

June sighs. "Jack, everyone for two hundred miles knows; you never shut up about how *one time* you were all heroic."

"More than once," I say.

"Twice," June says. "Maybe."

"Three times, at least!"

Bardle slams his fist on the table—June and I shut right up. "I told you that the Louisville Slicer *must* be retrieved," he growls.

"We tried!" Quint protests.

I shake my head. "This is no good! She's one-third of the way to completing her plan. That's pretty far! If this were a TV show, one-third is like the first commercial. Things are underway! Happening fast! Can we find Evie and stop her from achieving Step Two?"

"Unfortunately," Bardle replies, "the page that shows Steps Two and Three has been torn out."

Quint groans again. "She *writes* in the library book and she *tears out pages*?! So foul . . ."

At that very moment, bright light *floods* Joe's Pizza, like some sort of high-beam cannon. I'm wondering if someone turned the Christmas tree lights on full blast, but when we run to the door, I see that it's not the Christmas tree lights at all. . . .

"Guys," I say. "We don't have to find Evie. She found us. . . ."

KA-SLAM!

137

chapter fourteen

Meathook *barrels* into the Town Square.

I see something hanging from either side of him. Two huge boxes . . .

Squinting, I see they are massive blue metal Dumpsters. They dangle and scrape the side of the creature. A headlight shines from Meathook's head.

I shield my eyes, squinting. The monster stops. The spotlight is now a searchlight. A moment later, with a loud *KA-KLANG*, the Dumpsters fall to the ground. Zombies come streaming out of them!

Two dozen zombies instantly fill the Town Square! Chaos comes with them. June snarls, "Getting tired of these guys. I'm taking the high ground. Meet me at the tree house."

"And I'm going to try out some knuckle attacks," Dirk says, flexing his wrist. "Courtesy of Evie Snark and her dork collection."

The sound of monster battle cries rings out— snarling and barking and heavy growls. Some of our monster friends wield weapons from their dimension, while others simply hurl the zombies.

"DON'T BEAT ON THE ZOMBIES TOO BAD!" I shout. "It's not *their* fault they're zombies!"

Suddenly, Quint wheels toward me. "Jack! Remember our identical costume ideas from *The Empire Strikes Back*?!"

"Yes," I say, and then I finish his thought, 'cause that's what best buddies can do. "Of course! We'll take out Evie and Meathook just like the rebels took out the Empire AT-ATs!"

"Rover!" Quint shouts out. "Come here, furry friend!"

An instant later, Rover is charging around the corner. I grab his hide and pull myself into his armored seat. And I stub my toe. It's weird: end of the world, you don't think stubbing your toe would be a thing anymore. But it is.

Rover's butt plops into the snow, allowing Quint to scramble up onto the back.

"Reach into Rover's saddlebag!" I say. "I've got my supercharged T-shirt blaster in there!"

Rover races past our Christmas tree. I reach out and snag a long string of lights. The bulbs *tink* and *clink* as they bang together.

"Quint!" I shout excitedly. "This is *totally* like *The Empire Strikes Back*! We've got snow and everything. I'm Luke, steering the ship. And you're like Dak, firing the tow cable!"

Quint's response is short and not-so-sweet. "Dak dies, Jack."

Oh. Right. In that case . . .

Never mind! This is nothing like *The Empire Strikes Back*! Not at all! Now fire that light-bulb harpoon cable, buddy!

Icy water mixes with sweat and pours down my face. This enemy is *inside our town*. I scowl and urge Rover on, charging full-throttle.

The monster's legs are like an obstacle in a racing game—just need to thread the needle. I feel Quint bouncing in the seat, shaking the saddle. "Steady the harpoon!" I shout. "I'm making a pass!"

Rover runs harder, we're *bursting* through Meathook's legs, and I hear Quint fire. . . .

I glance back. I see the string of lights snapping in the air and then—THWACK!—the harpoon slams into Meathook's scaly hide.

"Great shot, Quint!" I shout, and then I'm jerking on Rover's reins, steering him around the rear of the huge monster. I smile, thinking, *Wait until that evil geek Evie realizes she was defeated by Star Wars tactics!*

Rover whoops. The string of lights circles and tightens. Meathook's next step is an awkward lurch. Snow erupts as his hand thumps the street.

"The monster's legs are totally tangled!" I shout. "It's gonna fall!"

Everyone braces themselves.

But this isn't Star Wars. This is just a dumb Jack Sullivan plan. Meathook simply steps *through* the string of lights, and—

POP! POP POP. The bulbs shatter, then—

RIP! Our bootleg harpoon cord tears.

"Foiled!" Quint yells. The T-shirt cannon is jerked from his hands. It flies past me. Then the string of lights circles around me. My butt's *jerked* from the seat.

"Not good!" I shout as I spin and twirl.

My stomach flips as Meathook's head jerks, whipping me around. I get a glimpse of snow, and then wood: the tree house ledge.

I'm swinging toward it. I reach out, hoping to grab it—because if I swing back, it'll be directly *into the monster's mouth*. And I *sort of* grab it, but mostly it's June grabbing *me*. She's up in the tree house—and her hand snags mine, catching me in mid-air.

"Get up here!" June barks, yanking me up onto the icy tree house deck. Meathook snarls. And that's when I see it.

The Louisville Slicer. Evie's carrying it. . . .

I don't hesitate. "June, it's Sled-Shot time."

"We don't have a sled anymore. That dude ate it!"

"I'M THE SLED NOW!" I shout. I climb into the Sled-Shot. June reluctantly wheels the massive launcher around, aiming me like some sort of human howitzer.

I see the Louisville Slicer, its sharp tip bobbing against the night sky. Evie's fingers are tight around the handle.

I glance back at June, and I shout, "NOW!"

She fires the Sled-Shot—which contains only me, and—

I'm gonna land on top of that big monster. And then I bet it'll be a cool thing where I'll be standing and Evie's standing and we're maintaining perfect balance atop the monster while we shout cool lines back and forth.

But instead—

OOF!

It does not go well.

I'm immediately slipping off the monster's back. I'm on all fours, trying to hang on. I'm so terrified that I just beg. "Lady, give me back my blade!" I cry.

"Wish that I could, little buddy!" she says cheerfully. "But I'm afraid I have big plans for it. Villainous plans."

"Don't call me little buddy!" I growl. My boots are scraping and kicking Meathook's hardened hide, looking for a foothold. My hand slips, fingers pawing the monster's wet skin. "And we *know* you have big plans for the Louisville

Slicer," I say. "'Cause you're a *lunatic* and you're obsessed with a whole *cabal of lunatics*."

Just then, I hear Dirk howl. And as he does, Evie's ears sort of perk up. Like she's *happy* my buddy might be hurt.

Evie grabs my coat and pulls me close. She whispers triumphantly: *"In one moment, I'll have all that I need. And then Ghazt will be here. As easy as A-B-C. . . ."*

Just then, a pair of zombies *soars* past our heads. Like, airborne undead. We both pause—

Um.
Weird.

Yeah, that was honestly unexpected.

147

Another zombie sails past us. Its pinwheeling arms nearly take Evie's head off. Evie ducks, dropping me. A quick scream escapes my lungs—then I'm falling.

I see swirling white below, mixed with blurs and flashes of zombie action. My arms spin, tumbling, soaking-wet winter coat like a giant anchor, and—

SPLONK!

A mound of fresh, wet snow breaks my fall.

Sitting up, I see the source of the soaring zombies: the hammock I strung up on Kylnn's spikes! It's basically a giant ZOMBIE SLINGSHOT! Zombies are snagged in the massive mesh.

"COME HAVE ME!" Skaelka shouts, egging on the zombie horde from atop a snow mound. The ghastly mass charges toward my ax-wielding friend. Skaelka dodges, and the zombies tumble forward, into the slingshot—

"Again, Biggun!" Skaelka shouts. "LET FLY!"

Biggun pulls back the hammock bed, then—
TWANG!

The hammock hurls more zombies. They twist and spin and sail toward Evie.

Evie is nearly knocked from atop Meathook by a soaring zombie. But she hangs on—and the foul duo disappears into the swirling snow. . . .

It's over. For now. I'm catching my breath, heaving, when I see it. Stuck to a broken, icy streetlamp, where Evie nearly fell.

A piece of paper clings to the cracked ice. I step closer—it's the missing page from *Interdimensional Terrors: A History of the Cabal of the Cosmic*. . . .

chapter fifteen

The page is snow-soaked, but mostly intact.

My hands are shaking from the cold—but it's also more that that. I'm quivering because this is BIG.

This can tell us WHY Evie stole the Slicer!

I spot Bardle and Quint standing beneath the old Buffalo Wing joint. "Hey, knowledgeable buddies!" I shout as I race toward them. "Look! The missing page from the library book!"

Bardle's long fingers take the page. I watch his eyes scan it. Bardle's pupils don't go back and forth when he reads—they just keep going, disappearing at one side of the eye, reappearing on the other. Like they move in a circle. It's super unnerving, no lie. . . .

What he says, though, and what I see—it's even more unnerving. . . .

STEP TWO: CAPTURE AN UNDEAD HUMAN BEING. THE HUMAN MIND IS A COMPLEX THING, SO GHAZT REQUIRES A FRESHLY ZOMBIFIED BODY TO ENTER. THE SIMPLIFIED BRAIN WORKINGS OF THE UNDEAD MAKE A ZOMBIE THE PERFECT VESSEL.

STEP THREE: PLACE THE ARTIFACT IN THE ZOMBIFIED HUMAN'S HANDS TO OPEN A PORTAL, ALLOWING GHAZT TO ENTER THE ZOMBIFIED BODY. GHAZT WILL THEN TAKE CONTROL OF THAT PERSON'S BODY. FOREVER.

Those words repeat in my head: *FRESHLY ZOMBIFIED BODY.*

I heard Dirk cry out. And I don't see him.

Suddenly there's this tight, burning, *screaming* feeling in my chest. I want to puke, right there in the snow. But I don't. Instead, I'm turning, leaving, even as I hear my friends calling after me.

Evie trapped us in her house and tried to zombify us. But we outsmarted her. *Our* geekiness defeated *her* geekiness.

Only she wasn't done. She needed a *new zombie.* She came back, head-on, into Wakefield Town Square. I thought we defeated her. But now I'm afraid I'm wrong. . . .

I'm marching across the Town Square. My head is snapping from side to side, quick looks, scanning, searching. Monster friends are rising, checking each other for injuries. No serious wounds.

I come to the tree house.

I'm grabbing the ladder.

Climbing.

Heart slamming. Palms sweaty. Pulling myself over the side.

I find him . . .

"Dirk?"

He doesn't respond.

"Hey, buddy," I say softly. "You OK?"

After a long moment, he shrugs. "Nah. I'm not."

My heart stops slamming, because the fear of not knowing is over. Now it's just coldness. It's cold on my insides, spreading outward.

"I messed up," Dirk says. "I got sloppy."

I slowly step forward. I see it.

The wound is on his forearm. Just a tiny drop of blood. But it's a zombie bite, just the same.

Dirk is calm. "Nothing to do, bro. I know you want to save the day—but you can't. Then you'll feel lousy—like you failed. Here's a Dirk secret: *If you don't try, you can't fail.* My old man taught me that."

153

I get right in his face—closer than anyone has probably *ever* gotten in Dirk's face before. Or if they did, they left with their face looking a bit mangled.

"Buddy," I say. "I would *love* to belt out a big, over-the-top, movie-type speech right now all about how much I love you and all the reasons I won't let you get zombified. But there's no time. Right now—there's only time for *fixing you*."

CLANK, CLANK, CLANK.

Our pulley conveyor. I see Bardle step from the lift basket, followed by June and Quint.

They see Dirk, they see my face—and they know.

"We must act quickly," Bardle says. His voice is barely a whisper.

Dirk doesn't resist. Moments later, he's stretched out on our poker table. . . .

I expect it to be like a scene from one of those TV shows with doctors running around emergency rooms. You know the ones, where they spend like half their time saving lives and the other half making out in hospital closets? Those shows were always on in the background at the different foster homes I lived in.

But here, now, no one freaks out.

Life's funny like that. The times when you want to freak out the most—those are the times when you can't freak out at all.

"Urghhh . . ." Dirk groans. Bardle examines the wound. He checks Dirk's pulse. And he does things I've never seen a human doctor do—he feels Dirk's hair, he inspects his fingernails, he measures the lines in his hands.

After a long moment, Bardle looks up.

Bardle doesn't get to respond. Because the tree house explodes.

At least, that's what it feels like. One moment, the far wall is there—the next, it's gone. Splinters hang in the air. Dust rolls.

It's Evie. And Meathook. They have returned.

Meathook's tongue lashes out and jabs forward—

One second Dirk is lying in front of us.
The next, the table has toppled over and he's
dangling in the air.

Meathook turns. I get one last glimpse. . . .

Dirk, sagging, spinning, hanging from the
monster's tongue. His eyes catch mine. His
mouth opens. I can just barely hear him over
the howling wind. . . .

"It's OK, guys. It's OK. . . ."

chapter sixteen

I'm frozen for a moment. Then I'm unstuck, running up to the tree house ice ball cannon launcher. I need to fight back. I need to stop her!

But it's too late.

Evie and Meathook are gone, disappeared into the snow.

Back downstairs. Moving quick. My hands slam the table. My voice jumps and spikes and it doesn't even sound like me. "Bardle, how do we fix Dirk? Just *tell me.*"

Bardle's face is blank. He doesn't know. I can see it. "There's nothing I can do. There's too little time."

I'm sorry, Bardle, but that answer won't work. Our friend is going to be a zombie.

Also, he's going to be used in an ancient ritual to open a portal and bring cosmic evil to Earth.

But mostly the zombie thing.

We need to stop Dirk from turning zombie!

Bardle brushes past me to the chalkboard I took from the elementary school months earlier. Our map of Wakefield is taped there.

Bardle points a long, thin finger at the map.

June leans forward. "The Christmas tree farm?" she asks.

"Huh? I don't even know what that *is*," I say.

"It's where people could go and chop down their own Christmas trees. *Before* the Monster

Apocalypse," Quint says. "Before you could simply grab whatever tree you liked, as we did."

"There's a creature there who perhaps could help," Bardle says. "A monster named Warg."

"Warg . . ." I repeat. I'm thinking back to our ice fishing failure. "Wait, Skaelka mentioned a Warg! Oh, man, we don't have to, like, *slay this creature*, do we? Like, because Warg's green monster blood cures zombieness or something?"

For a second, I think Bardle is going to laugh. But this isn't any sort of moment for laughing. "Slay her?" Bardle asks. "Oh, no, you will not slay her—I promise you that. You could not if you tried."

"Skaelka said Warg was 'One not in the community,'" June comments. "'One that does not matter.'"

"Did you guys kick her out?" I ask Bardle. Bardle scoffs. "She exiled *herself*. She has no interest in contributing to our community. For that reason, I do not think she will help you. But—she is your only chance."

I nod. We're desperate.

And when you're desperate, your only chance is the chance you take.

The monsters watch us leave town. Their heads are rolled back, skyward. That's like the monster version of sad head-hanging. I learned that when I mistakenly knocked over our milkshake tower.

Bardle stops us at the edge of town. "You should know . . ." Bardle says, "based on the size of Dirk's bite, he has three Earth hours. After that, he will no longer be Dirk. He will no longer be your friend. He will no longer be human. . . ."

Quint reaches down and sets a timer on his *Back to the Future* watch. It beeps.

Three hours to save our friend's life. . . .

Then we'll just have to be quick. . . .

The Christmas tree farm is beyond the train tracks. A thin layer of frost covers every inch of ground. We stomp in, following a winding path through the woods.

Up ahead, beyond the fir trees, I can make out a big red barn. Its doors are just barely open. We approach a metal fence covered in ice. I grab hold and shake it. Ice cracks. Normally, Dirk would just rip through this. But we don't have that help now.

Instead, we climb over it. Land hard. Feet crunching on icy grass

Quint looks at me. "We need Warg's *help*. Don't forget. Just help. Nothing else, Jack!"

I frown. "Why do I feel like that comment was intended for me?"

"Because I was staring at you when I said it and the last word in the comment was *Jack*."

"What he means," June says, "is that we *don't* need to get into a whole big monster battle, here. Just find out how to save Dirk—and get out. Don't go instigating!"

I roll my eyes. "I don't instigate. When have I *ever* instigated a big monster battle?"

June cocks her head. "Jack. . . ."

Times Jack Instigated a Monster Battle!

"Fine," I grumble. "I won't instigate."

The tree farm stretches out in front of us. I see thousands of Christmas trees, arranged in long, perfectly ordered rows. But they haven't been trimmed, of course, and are now a bit overgrown. These Christmas trees will never be used for their intended purpose. I look at

June. She's thinking the same thing I am. It's a bummer—but at least we got *our* Christmas.

Then she whispers, "Guys, look."

Something is rolling toward us along the path. It leaves a smooth path in the thin snow.

"It looks like a bowling ball," Quint says, "made of mucus."

As it spins to a stop, I realize. . . .

"Guys, I've *seen* this before," I whisper. "On our way to ice fishing. I thought it was, like, some monstrous critter—but it's . . ."

It's a reminder of just how bizarre the world is now that the sight of a rolling, gooey, eyeball creature only *medium* weirds us out.

The eyeball rocks back, then forward. And then it tilts to the side, looking beyond us.

June says, "It's like it's checking to see if anyone else is coming."

"It's just us, dude," I say. "We're the whole adventure party."

And then more eyeballs show up, coming from every direction. Nearly a hundred, tumbling through the trees. The biggest are like beach balls, the smallest aren't much larger than a peanut M&M.

Soon, we're surrounded. . . .

Wargball?
Eyewarg?

chapter seventeen

The eyeballs turn to look at one another—which is, yes, as weird as it sounds. And then—

THEY SWARM! "I don't think this is a welcome party!" June shouts.

They're tumbling over one another, bounding and jumping from all sides. One clings to my back. Another is on my shoulder. "Run!" I shout.

"Run? Really?" June asks. "Good plan, Jack. I thought we should stay put and cuddle up with the eyeball army!"

"No time for battle banter, friends!" Quint exclaims. "FLEE THE EYEBALL ARMY!"

We quickly get separated, and I'm soon lost in a maze of trees. At every turn, I see only pine needles and eyeballs—eyeballs rolling and bouncing toward me. More leap at me, sticking to my clothes. They're unstoppable. I swat one away—then two more leap.

Suddenly, I'm pushing through thick needles and stumbling out into a small clearing. The barn is ahead. A rusted tractor sits next to it, half-buried beneath snow. I see a sign for Christmas tree decorations.

"EYEBALL HORDE!" June shouts. I glance over and see her burst through the trees.

"IN HOT PURSUIT!" Quint cries out, following.

The barn's two doors are open just wide enough for us to, maybe, fit through. . . .

"In there!" I cry, and we speed across the snow. I burst through the barn doors. My shoulders scrape against the wood. Splat sounds echo as the eyeballs are knocked off.

We spill onto the cold, straw-covered ground.
The eyeballs scatter as we stand. A light dusting
of snow is sprinkled on the barn floor. It's dark—
just a few thin shafts filtering through cracks in
the wood beam walls and the high ceiling.

More eyeballs follow through the door—but
they don't attack. They're waiting for something.

From the far-corner darkness comes the
sound of shuffling feet and slime.

I squint—and see a monster that's like a weird,

saggy, fleshy sack. "It's like a big booger with feet," June whispers.

One of those feet *stomps* the floor. At once the eyeballs roll toward her. They leap up, covering her like some coat of peeping pupils.

We are looking at . . .

The barn shudders in the wind. My voice is shaky. "Our friend was bit by a zombie. And we were told you can help us."

Warg speaks in a raspy whisper. "Who?"

"Um. Dirk. Dirk Savage. You probably don't know him."

"Who told you I could help you?" Warg asks.

"Oh. Right. Bardle."

Warg laughs. It's a sandpaper-and-broken glass sound. "He was wrong."

Every one of Warg's eyeballs blinks in unison. I realize they're all interconnected. Part of one another. "Leave," Warg says. "I will not help you. I have learned it is best *not* to get involved in the affairs of others."

I rock slowly in place. My chest is tight. Hands shaking. Leaving is not an option. Warg has something. Some knowledge, some cure, something that can help us.

June growls. "Listen up. We demand you help us. You came to our world and you brought a zombie plague and now that zombie plague is gonna end my friend's life. So like I said—HELP US!"

The monster sighs.

Somewhere, Dirk is hurting—and all the monster can do is *sigh*.

I'm suddenly racing forward, with no plan. All I have is a deep, furious WANT to save my friend. Because soon, Dirk will be lost *forever*.

"YOU HAVE TO HELP US!" I cry out. "YOU WILL—"

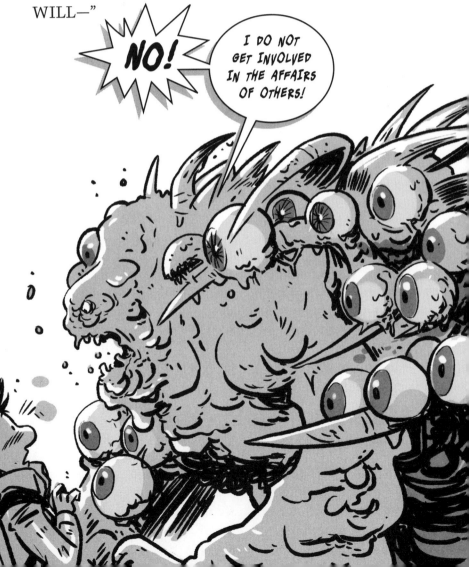

RAZOR-SHARP JABBERS erupt from Warg's back, piercing eyeballs like a skewer.

The eyeballs split open—every one, at once. They don't *roar* but instead release a strange, high-pitched shriek.

It is Warg, howling—and the sound comes *through* the eyeballs.

It turns my blood cold. We all stagger back, terrified. We tumble out, through the doorway, to the cold ground, as—

CLANG!

The heavy barn doors shut. It is a thunderous clap, bouncing off the trees, ricocheting around my skull, then fading into infinity. . . .

And that sound.

That slam.

It's like hearing the doors slam shut on Dirk.

Quint places his hand on my shoulder, trying to make me feel like it's OK. But when he puts his hand there, I see his *Back to the Future* watch, counting down the seconds . . . the seconds until Dirk is lost forever.

We're almost out of time. And we're not getting *closer* to our goal—we're getting further and further!

That's not how it's supposed to work.

In the distance, I see the Christmas lights in Town Square. The bulbs, all lit up. And I realize . . .

Warg has a *perfect* view of our town. Our *community*. I first saw her eyeballs when we began planning Christmas. Warg was watching us from up here.

Skaelka said Warg's not part of the community. But maybe she wants to be?

Maybe she was watching because she felt that feeling that's the *worst* of all feelings. That feeling of being, like, *left out*?

I don't know the history of Warg and the other monsters. Maybe if we save Dirk, and we all live to fight another day—I'll learn. All I know, right now, is that for some reason, Warg cares enough to watch, at least.

I leap to my feet, scoop up a snowball, and hurl it at the barn. . . .

I know you've been watching the town! Bardle told us you wanted to be alone! But we're not gonna let you.

Because it's Christmas! It's the time for helping!

June looks at me with a sad smile and gently squeezes my hand. "Jack's right! The holidays are not the time for spying from far away like a weirdo! It's not the time for letting kids get zombified! It's a time for helping, and being good! SO HELP US!"

Quint hurls a snowball. And another.

I heave and heave. It's cold, but I'm soaked in sweat from the fear and the screaming.

I picture Dirk. His face changing. His body morphing. And there's nothing I can do.

"Look," I say. "If you want to spy on us—fine. But enjoy it while you can. 'Cause soon, there won't be any town to spy on. You might not want to get involved in the affairs of others— but the fact is, there's a bad dude who's going to bring Ghazt to this world! And Ghazt's going to get *very* involved."

That's when the barn door opens.

Warg steps out. Every single eyeball blinks. Her voice is a wet snarl. "Did you say Ghazt?"

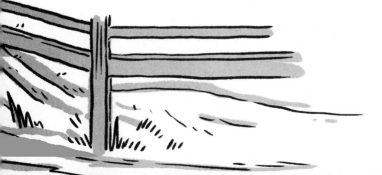

chapter eighteen

I KNOW GHAZT. I KNOW THE CREATURE'S POWER. AND YES, I WATCH THE TOWN.

YOU ARE CORRECT—THE TOWN WILL BE GONE IF GHAZT COMES HERE.

"Wait, hold up, really?" I say. "I was just saying that in hopes of getting you out there."

Warg's head dips. Frost dots her strange, loose face. "Your town will be overrun by the undead. An endless army. Ghazt is G̨ęĹ́nī. The *General*. The General of the undead."

June stammers. "You mean . . . he, like, leads zombies?"

"Not leads," Warg says. *"Controls."*

Now I understand why Evie had thousands upon thousands of zombified action figures. It was her way of planning, plotting. . . .

And I understand, now, why Evie wants Ghazt, specifically. Why she's not content with the Cosmic Servants already on Earth, why she's not just trying to bring Ṛeżžöcħ himself here. Because she wants something that can control the thousands and thousands of zombies.

"Take this," Warg says. She plucks a single eyeball from her body and pushes it into my hands. "These globular organs are why Bardle sent you."

YOUR FRIEND MUST DRINK THE JELLY-FILLED CENTER BEFORE HE IS FULLY UNDEAD. THAT WILL REVERSE THE ZOMBIFICATION.

Wait. What? No way.

As I'm holding the eyeball, I realize I only thought this far. I only thought about *figuring out* how to get Dirk fixed.

And where do we go now? Where did she take him?

Her house, right?

But I'm not so sure.

She *brought the Louisville Slicer with her.* Home is where she kept it! And she needs to be with the artifact in order to carry out her nefarious plan. . . .

Quint's watch is *tick, tick, tick*ing. And there's no way to stop it. No way to stop time. The moment the zombie bit Dirk, things got rolling.

I can hear her voice, ringing in my head: *"In one moment, I'll have all that I need. And then Ghazt will be here. As easy as A-B-C. . . ."*

I spin around.

"The ABC Block Smasher Cinema! *That's* where she's taking Dirk. That's where this is all going down. I'm sure of it."

June's jaw is tight. She sighs. "That is miles from here. Many hours of walking. . . ."

My heart pounds. *No way. No way.* We didn't make it this far to *not* finish. I mean—I've got an oversized *eyeball* in my hand. You don't waste oversized eyeballs!

But June's right. We're miles from our
destination. We need, like, a . . .

"Christmas miracle," June says, softly—and
she points. . . .

And there I see Bardle,
Skaelka, and Rover
running toward us.
Our own Christmas
miracle.

It's a card. June's hands tremble as she
opens it. Quint peers closer. I read over their
shoulders.

June, Quint—

Merry Christmas! I feel lousy that you have to wait until spring to answer the radio call. If you want to get to the big city and try to find your family, you should get to do it now.

So I built this.

I'm not sure what Jack's gonna do—but I'm staying put. I fit here. Hard to explain.

I didn't know it, yet, when we were planning to leave. But the holidays showed me. I have better friends here than I ever had before the Monster Apocalypse.

I'll finish the engine this week! Promise, guys.

Merry Christmas!

Dirk

Mobile hot chocolate station

I look up. I don't totally understand. Behind me, Quint and June are in shock.

I look in Rover's eyes. And then I notice something in his mouth—a big giant Dozer bone. And attached to that bone—rope! Like an old-timey sled dog! And I see what he's pulling.

"It's Big Mama!" I say.

"But Big Mama isn't Big Mama anymore," June says. "She's like—Sled Mama! Or the Big Sled!"

Quint grins. "No, no, I got it. She is . . ."

– SNOW MAMA! –

Ice ball cannon

Dozer Hide Steering Wheel Cover (thanks Skaelka!)

Carrabullis skull, for scaring off zombies (a long story for another time)

Rover reins

Frostile Fur Seat Covers — warm and cozy!

Anti-ice snow chains

Shock absorber

Super slick ski-treads

"Dirk built this—so that we could leave," June says. "So we could make it all the way to New York. . . ."

Dirk had made up his mind. He would stay. He found community here. A home. More than he ever had during the world before. I never realized how much Dirk is like me. "Guys, we have to save Dirk," I say. "Right now."

Bardle and Skaelka climb down from the sled. Skaelka eyes Warg suspiciously. Warg returns the look. They don't high-five or hug, that's for sure. But I see something there—an understanding that Warg gave us what we needed. And that means something.

"C'mon, Jack." It's June, tugging at my sleeve.

"Rover, buddy!" I say, giving him a scratch behind his wet ears. "You ready to tow your radical hero buds?"

He's panting—two hard fumes of monstrous dog breath rush from his nose. Then a toothy smile. I hop in the front. June climbs in beside me. Quint piles in the back.

"Let's do this," I say, pulling gently at the reins. Rover trots forward. Big Mama's massive frame jerks. As we approach the edge of the Christmas tree farm, I look back.

The monsters are watching us go. I throw Warg, Bardle, and Skaelka a wave. Then we're off—and I'm trying to prepare myself for what's to come. I glance back at Quint's watch:

Now only forty-seven minutes remaining—
forty-seven minutes until he's Dirk no more. . . .
By the time we get to him, he'll be nearly all
zombie. He won't look like Dirk.
I've seen hundreds of zombies since the
Monster Apocalypse began, months back. I
shut my eyes, and I can picture some of them—
undead faces flashing across the back of
my eyelids. . . .

The faces were scary at first. The strange,
broken bodies. I got used to it. But to see my *friend*
like that? I'm not sure if I'll be able to take it. . . .

I've learned that how you deal with this stuff, how you face it—it all comes from how you *think about it.* When the Monster Apocalypse began, I couldn't think about it like a monster apocalypse. I couldn't think about the end of the world. Because that's just so bananas overwhelming that I would have curled up into a ball and rocked back and forth until I faded away to nothing!

So, I created Feats of Apocalyptic Success—I looked at my new life, my new world, like a video game. Something to be beaten. A big crazy land to explore and to conquer!

And I do that now. Trying to shift my mind out of "my buddy Dirk is less than an hour away from becoming a *zombie*" mode to "we're about to sneak into a villain's fortress and be super-awesome heroes straight out of a great adventure story!" mode.

And I have to admit—I'm feeling like Santa Claus as I tug the reins on Snow Mama. But I'm not off to deliver gifts. *I'm off to deliver PAIN!*

Actually, sorry—that's a little too hard-core. I thought it sounded cool in my head. I'm off to RESCUE MY BUDDY AND GET BACK MY BLADE!

"Hey, friend," Quint says, tapping my shoulder and pointing. "What's that?"

I squint. "I'm not sure. . . ."

June's jaw drops. She manages, "I can't believe it's real. Dirk wasn't crazy. It's straight out of one of his *Conan the Barbarian* fantasies."

I cry out, "FROST GIANT! Hang on tight!"

Rover's paws slide, and then he's leaping, tumbling into the front of the sled, as Quint tugs and—

Snow Mama spins out. We're slicing across a snowbank, leaving the Frost Giant behind, then up, landing atop a long sheet of cars, when I see it—

ABC BLOCK SMASHER CINEMA! A movie theater that feels like it's some sort of castle belonging to an ultra-villain. And only a true, pure, ultimate geek would use a movie theater as a headquarters.

It was summer when the Monster Apocalypse started. And summer's when the big movies come out.

"It seems a large number of people were enjoying the air-conditioning on the day of the apocalypse," Quint says. "Because the parking lot is quite full!"

He's right. Zombies galore. Rover lowers his head and pulls us, scraping over the roofs of cars and up the steps to the entrance.

Vine-Thingies have grown up the front of the theater. They're usually dangerous, vicious plant monsters—but they're frozen now. *Everything* is frozen.

I'm awed by the sight. A movie theater has become the fortress of a great villain—and we now must step into it to rescue a friend and retrieve an epic weapon.

For a second, I forget about the danger and think only of the awesomeness. It's June that thaws me from my frozen awe. She elbows me. Her lips are blue and tight as she nods. No question. It's time.

chapter nineteen

The front of the towering theater is a wall of broken glass. Sheets of ice and frozen Vine-Thingies hold it all together.

"Wait here, Rover," I say. "We'll be back. I think . . ."

We stomp over mounds of snow and duck beneath icicles as we enter the lobby.

"Great . . ." June says. "It's frozen horror."

Half-frozen zombies fill the lobby. Their upper bodies move freely—but they don't stagger or skulk or shamble. They're stuck. . . .

Some crowd. . . .

Everything smells like drenched dogs.

But there's another smell, too.

The movie theater smell.

The floor is a sheet of ice, a foot thick. Peering through, I see old ticket stubs and bits of popcorn and icy Goobers on the floor. It's like some preserved *Jurassic Park* frozen-in-time scene of the theater before the world ended.

The smell never left. It's baked into the walls.

Can I say something? The movie theater is my favorite place on earth. It's the one place where I could always go and just, like, shut down. The lights dim and you dig into popcorn—and you just get *lost*. Butter drips through the bag and stains your shirt and chocolate melts on your jeans but it's OK, because it's the movies.

Movies are escape.

Escape from the cruddy parts of everyday life.

But now I'm amid the cruddiest part of my weird everyday life—and it's happening in my *temple*.

I growl. "Evie has taken my happiest place— and turned it against me!"

Quint pats my shoulder. "I know, friend. I know. . . ."

We pass huge standees for movies that have been filmed but will never be released. Water drips and the cardboard sags.

I realize: There are completed movies, sitting there, in a Hollywood basement somewhere! They'd better be preserved correctly! If the world ever returns to normal and I discover there's some secret, unseen director's cut of *Iron Man 3* that got "lost"—well, let's just say I won't be happy. . . .

Gimme those lost movies!

Quint snaps me out of it. "Jack, are you thinking about the movies you'll never see?"

"No," I lie. "Maybe. Maybe no. Maybe yes. What if—"

June says, "Dude! Don't get distracted. We have to be laser-focused. We are in DIRK WILL SOON BE A ZOMBIE danger!"

June suddenly stops. "Tracks," she says, pointing to the floor. We see two pairs of fresh, snowy footprints across the icy carpet. One pair is staggered—like the person was becoming more and more undead as they walked. Dirk.

"Good," I say. "I wasn't wrong. They're here."

We follow the tracks to the second level of the three-story theater. We check each theater. Every time, it's like opening up the doors to a big room full of horror. Zombies shamble about, moaning hungrily.

June checks a theater. "No Dirk!" she calls. "Just zombies."

Quint checks a theater. "Same! No Dirk! Just zombies!"

I check a theater. "Nothing but more zombies!"

Soon, only one theater remains: the biggest of them all. The IMAX.

I'm about to charge in, when June points to a half-open door. "That goes to the balcony."

We climb the winding steps. My bag bounces against my leg. "Guys, I know this isn't the time," I whisper, "but I've never watched a movie from a balcony. I always wanted to."

"Let's hope this movie has a happy ending," June says, and she pushes the door open. We step out onto the balcony: a few hundred seats, overlooking another thousand seats below. And the massive IMAX screen towering up ahead.

There's only one person in the audience.

Dirk.

He's at the very center seat. And he sits there.
Perfectly still.

It's eerie. Creepy. Freaking *terrifying looking*.

And then Dirk moans. It's an awful combo
cry: a howling human and a groaning zombie,
mushed into one awful noise.

"I don't see Evie," June says. "Let's get down
there! Feed Dirk this eyeball and blow this
popsicle stand and forget about all this—"

But that's when I hear the snarl beneath us.

Meathook. The entire balcony quakes. I catch
a whiff of monstrous body odor, and then hot

breath as—But that's when we hear the snarl. It comes from below.

My heart jumps, my stomach rolls, and I'm suddenly thinking only of escape. A way out. Leaving this place and this moment.

It's Meathook. He is beneath us.

The balcony trembles and sways. I catch a whiff of evil body odor, and then hot breath blows over us . . .

Meathook emerges: rising up, bit by bit, until we're staring him right in the chops. His one massive paw swipes, slashing the air, engulfing me.

"His fat, stupid hand has me!" I holler, as I'm swung and—

"ARGH!" Quint cries. He's scooped up, too. Our heads clonk together and my world spins.

It's a blurry mess, but I get a glimpse of June leaping over a seat, trying to get away. But the beast's tongue SNAPS out and plucks her.

In just moments . . .

chapter twenty

My winter action outfit's hood tugs at me. It's tight around my throat. I manage to loosen it, so I can breathe better. And just in time to gasp—

The curtains open with a *whoosh*, revealing the IMAX screen. Far below, I see a figure, stepping from the darkness. . . .

Evie taps the Louisville Slicer against the seats as she walks along the front row. My heart growls—I mean, heart growling isn't a thing, but that's basically what happens. I'm raging on the inside as I watch her grip the thing she stole and used to set this all off! My blade! My weapon!

We watch, helpless, as Evie approaches Dirk.

She places the Louisville Slicer in his hands and wraps his fingers around the handle. Evie looks to the screen.

"Ghazt!" Evie calls out. Her voice is high—excited but nervous. "It is time, my general."

Silence for a moment. And then Evie shrieks—she shrieks in the language of Reżżóch.

"€ ł*úúĘXIŖş űŹj ĢdfDĹńd!"

The awful words hang in the stillness of the theater. Then—

An ear-splitting CRACK erupts and every single speaker booms.

I gulp. "I guess Ghazt heard her. . . ."

Behind us, the projector hums to life. A bright white light showers the screen.

Dirk is silhouetted in shadow below, holding up the blade. Hanging from Meathook, I can just make out the side of Dirk's face. It is a mask of undead features. Dirk must be about . . .

– 94% zombie! –

Evie turns, flashing me a smile. "Jack," she says. "This must really eat you up inside. *Your* weapon. *Your* friend. Being used to usher ancient cosmic evil into *your* world. You're kinda lousy at being a hero, aren't you?"

The massive IMAX screen is suddenly a swirling pool: dark colors splashing and neon streaks glowing. It's like liquid metal.

Light bursts and flashes on the screen. It has a *power* to it—I feel my hair blow back, like I'm looking into the eye of a swirling storm.

I see flashing images—like zooming at hyperspeed through a string of galaxies. Worlds and dimensions—things my mind can't even comprehend. And I can do nothing but watch.

"Guys," I whisper. "Her plan is nearly complete. All three steps . . ."

I don't think Meathook likes us chatting—'cause he suddenly *swings* us into the balcony ledge. Sharp pain shoots through my belly. There's something daggering into my side. I reach into my pocket, and I realize—

The zombie action figures! The custom ones that Evie made! It's the height of geekiness. The peak of everything I love. The peak of, in my mind, *good*.

"Hey, Evie!" I shout.

That gets Evie's attention.

She walks up the sloping aisle. Meathook's head dips, lowering us toward her. I shove the handful of figures forward. It's like I'm holding out a crucifix to ward off a vampire. But my goal is the opposite—I'm trying to draw her closer.

"Your thoughts betray you, Evie," I say. "I feel the good in you. The conflict."

"Don't quote *Return of the Jedi* to me!" she barks.

"But it's true!" I exclaim.

She shakes her head. "Not true! There is no conflict! NONE!"

But I see struggle in Evie's eyes. She's going to be convinced. She reaches out. Her fingers wrap around the figures. . . .

"I understand you, Evie," I say. "You watched movies and read comics and you hoped that one day *you'd* get to experience real adventure! I'm the same! And now, we get to do it!"

She looks up, into my eyes. We *are* the same.

"Don't fight against us; join us!" I say. "We can hang out! You don't have to be alone in this big monstrous world! We've got a—um—like a—"

"A community!" Quint says.

"A community is even better than a Cosmic Cabal!" I tell her.

"Especially during the holidays!" June says. "And you're welcome to join! We're even having a Christmas bash! You're invited!"

YEOOO-WELLLL!

From the broken speakers comes a deafening,

inhuman, unearthly *WAIL*. A voice bellows:
"WHO. HAS SUMMONED. ME?"

Evie stiffens. The look in her eyes—the hint
of good—it has evaporated. "Yes, Jack. I watched
movies and read graphic novels and lost myself
in books. Like you. And I hoped that *one day*
I'd get real adventure. Like you. But there's one
important difference."

She *hurls* the action figures to the floor. "I
always rooted for the bad guy. . . ."

And I
won't be alone.
Soon, I will
help to lead
an **army**. . . .

She is lost to us.

And in my ear, I hear Dirk moaning. Time is running out.

A creature, a *being*, is appearing on-screen. Swirling from the darkness. Taking shape. A voice booms—but this time it doesn't come from the speakers. It comes from the *screen*.

"I AM GHAZT, SCOURGE OF THE COSMOS, GENERAL OF THE UNDEAD. I SERVE ONLY REZZÓCH. WHOM DO YOU SERVE?"

Evie is frozen for a moment. Her voice cracks at first, then she shouts, "You! I serve you! And you *are* a scourge! A scourge indeed! And a great general! Look—look what I have prepared! You're gonna love it!"

Evie hurries toward Dirk. She pats his shoulder. "Ghazt!" she calls out. "In moments, this human boy will become a zombie! And in that instant, you will take over his body! So you can do your general stuff here, in this dimension! On Earth!"

"Well . . ." June says, with a heavy sigh, "this is officially the worst Christmas ever."

"Wait!" I whisper. "CHRISTMAS! My gift!"

I think back to when June and I first talked about this. . . .

I glance upward. Meathook is fully entranced by the swirling action on screen. More than entranced—*spellbound*. Which is fair—I mean, Meathook is a Servant. Ghazt is a top-notch Cosmic Terror. I think Meathook is, like, starstruck. It's like if I went to Comic-Con and I met, I dunno, Daisy Ridley.

And the monster's starstruck-ness is to our benefit. "June," I whisper. "Can you reach into my bag?"

June cocks an eyebrow, skeptical—but she does it. She begins to pull her gift out. She half groans, half chuckles. "I still can't believe you made me wrap my own gift!"

"Open it," I say.

"Fine, fine."

"Hurry!"

"I'm trying!" June says.

"Why'd you have to wrap it so well?!" I mutter.

"YOU TOLD ME TO WRAP IT WELL!" June barks.

"Not now, you fools!" Quint exclaims. He reaches over, plucks one piece of yarn, and the whole thing basically unwraps itself. The shoebox top falls, and June peers inside—

She pulls her gift fully out—and sort of gasps as she sees it's the size of, like, Mega Man's Mega Buster or the arm cannon from Metroid. She slips it over her winter glove. . . .

It's everything, friend! Like a Swiss Army knife!

Full rundown later. For now, just do a Spider-Man wrist motion thing!

June looks at the gift. There's a quick moment—it has to be, because of the looming doom and impending horror—where she smiles.

She got what she wanted for Christmas.

And then her smile turns to a smirk. "Jack, I have *no clue* what 'a Spider-Man wrist motion thing' is."

"Sure you do! It's just, like, a little *fling fling*."

Somehow, amazingly, June understands what I mean by a little *fling fling* and she does a Spider-Man wrist motion and—

THWINK!

Holy cow! It's like that game! Assassin's Creed! Or Wolverine!

"Slice me!" I say as I swing my legs back, then forward, like pumping on a swing. June nods. "Save Dirk," she says, and—

CUT!

June slices off my winter hood, freeing me from Meathook's hold. I push off, like jumping from a swing. I land on the seat below, and then I'm leaping, seat to seat, and—

HEADS UP, GEEK! INCOMING NERD!

Or the other way around! Geek, nerd—

WHATEVER!

chapter twenty-one

"Miss me?" I shout as I crash-land on Evie's back.
It's a whole hero-villain piggyback situation. My
hands grasp her cloak.

"Get off!" she howls. She swipes and punches
and tries to toss me. But I just hang on tighter.
I'm annoying like that.

She lurches forward, toward Dirk.

I see my friend. His skin has turned gray. He's
almost completely undead.

As we stagger, Ghazt howls . . .

"HAVE YOU SUMMONED ME TO BRING ME UNTO
EARTH SO I MIGHT SERVE ʁEŻŻÖCH? IF NOT, YOU ARE
A FOOL—AND YOU WILL PAY."

Evie squirms. I'm high on her shoulder. She
tries to answer the monster. I throw my hand
over her mouth to stop her. She gets spit on my
palm. Gross!

We stagger back and forth. Slam into a seat. "Dirk, drop that bat!" I shout.

But his nearly zombified brain doesn't hear me. He just continues gripping it tight. Another staggering step, and then—*CRUNCH!* Evie steps onto one action figure. Then another.

"You're destroying your custom figures!" I cry. "IT CAN'T BE WORTH IT!"

Evie's lips twist into a smile. "Do you smell it? The energy in the air? You're too late, kid. . . ."

KA-KA-KRAK! I turn to see black lightning erupting from the screen. It zigzags toward the Louisville Slicer, toward Dirk!

"IT'S BEGINNING!" Quint cries, flashing his watch. "Ghazt's essence will travel that stream and into Dirk! WE'RE NEARLY OUT OF TIME!"

I hang on to Evie's back. My hand covers her mouth. "You can go back now, Ghazt! We're all good without you! No more lightning needed!"

But the swirling on-screen intensifies. This monster is going to travel into my friend!

"Evie," I growl. "When this is all done—if any of us are still here—we're gonna have words! But for now—I gotta handle my buddy!"

With that, I leap from her back and race through the theater. Down one row, vaulting over a seat, and then stumbling into Dirk. Black energy and heat radiates from the bat. Stepping toward Dirk is like stepping near a fire.

I see it. Up close.

My weapon. The Louisville Slicer.

It's time to take it back. I throw my hands around the handle and—

The bat shakes and trembles in my hands. Energy surges back and forth—a single stream that seems to move both ways, energy into the bat, and energy out, into the IMAX.

I look to the screen, and I shout, "OK, I have the bat now—and STOP ALL EVIL ACTIVITIES. I CONTROL THE BLADE AND I DECLARE, UM, YOU ARE NOT WELCOME IN THIS WORLD! Also . . . ṚEŻŻŐCH WORDS!"

I don't know any Ṛeżżőch words, so instead I just have to literally say, out loud, "ṚEŻŻŐCH WORDS."

It doesn't work.

Energy blasts through the bat! I'm hurled over a seat! And as I am, holding the bat, I *pull* Ghazt. The energy is like a rope, tugging him from the screen.

"Um. Guys," I cry out. "HOW DO I MAKE HIM *NOT* COME THROUGH?"

Evie screams, "STOP, YOU IDIOT BOY!" and she sounds terrified. "If you pull him out of there without a vessel ready to receive him—if Ghazt comes through the portal *for real*, as *himself*—the entire *world* will collapse. It's too much energy transference at once!"

"What are you talking about?" I shout.

Let me put this in words you'LL understand.
GHOSTBUSTERS! NEVER CROSS THE STREAMS. When Egon says, "Try to imagine aLL life as you know it stopping instantaneously, and every molecule in your body exploding at the speed of light."

But I'm *unable* to let go. The quaking handle is, like, *locked* inside my hands. I tug and pull and stagger backward, up the aisle.

As I stumble back, *I'm pulling the monster from the screen.*

Ghazt, in his cosmically monstrous form, is being drawn into this dimension.

It's like fishing—I've got a bite—but I seriously DON'T WANT THIS BITE. And Ghazt doesn't care about everyone dying, exploding, whatever. I mean, the foul demon has probably never even *seen Ghostbusters.*

I have only one choice.

Destroy the thing that started this. Destroy the Louisville Slicer.

For Evie, it's an artifact, just step number one in a three-step plan. For me, it's my most precious belonging. But that can't matter anymore. Right now, the only thing that matters is stopping Ghazt and saving Dirk.

I dig deep and summon every ounce of strength I have. And then—

The lightning STOPS. The blade is freed! It is no longer pulling Ghazt! In an instant, Ghazt is yanked back into the screen.

I'm hurled onto my back.

I lie there for a moment. Catching my breath. I look at the blade. It is NOT destroyed. But a crack appears: a narrow fracture darts from the Slicer's tip down into the handle. From the crack comes darkness—seeping, pouring darkness.

"What the huh?" I wonder.

And then the IMAX screen erupts.

ZZZ-KRAK!!

Black lightning shoots across the theater, carving it apart. It is uncontrolled! Untamed! Jagged cracks slice through the ceiling.

I hear a tremendous crack, a monstrous boom, and Meathook goes down. . . .

Meathook is half-buried! His eyes go blank. He is out *cold*.

June bursts from his grip, screaming, "EVERYONE! DOWN!"

She rushes past me, grabbing Dirk's wrist and somehow finding the strength to pull him behind a row of seats. I dive behind them, meeting Quint there. I watch Evie *hurl* herself to the aisle floor.

The lightning continues erupting from the screen! Zapping, zipping, winging, shrieking! The floor is carved open.

"Ghazt is looking for a body to enter!" Quint cries out.

A final, tremendous gasp of energy erupts from the screen and bounces around the theater like a laser sprung loose. And then—

KA-SLAM!

The furious, blinding beam *crashes* into the first row of seats. The seats explode.

And it stops.

I look to the screen. It's returning to normal. The black, inky darkness is fading away. Just a massive white canvas.

It's over.

All is quiet.

I slowly stand. The theater smells like overcooked s'mores. The energy has left smoking, red-hot zigzag slices in the ceiling and walls. It's like someone took a lightsaber saw to it. A speaker falls. Seats topple over.

There's a moan at my feet. Dirk!

"So is Ghazt, y'know, gone?" I ask. "Back into the screen? And into its dimension?"

Quint looks up. He nods. "I think so. . . ."

I stare across the theater at Evie. June follows my look and growls, "And what do we do with her?"

But before we can do anything—

GRRRRRRUMBLE . . .

The floor of the theater is trembling. Evie shakes her head. "It looks like Ghazt has found a body to enter after all."

I feel the ground swelling beneath my boots. Lifting. Shaking.

Something is under there.

An awful thought enters my mind. I'm afraid I know what vessel the monster has entered. . . .

chapter
twenty-two

"Hey, Quint, buddy—*why* did you say they closed the theater again?" Quint opens his mouth to tell me, but as he does, something *bursts* from the ground. Seats fly, ice cracks, and a horrible howl echoes.

A rat.

A rat the size of a school bus.

But it's not simply a vehicle-sized rodent. It's monstrous. *Something* has happened to it. . . .

One leg is gnarled plastic. A chunk of its face is gooey. It's chomping and slurping on—

"Oh gross," June says as she realizes. "It's Evie's action figures!"

This monster—part rat, part stretched and melted action-figure plastic—stomps toward us, revealing itself fully—

– GHAZT THE RAT BEAST! –

Cosmically bad intentions!

Giant action-figure limbs!

Strange, snapping, twitching tail

Ghazt's eyes are fully white. Blood-red energy dances over its body. It shakes its head, and bits of electricity fly off it—like a dog drying itself.

The monster steps forward. Its mouth narrowly opens, but out comes not a hiss or a growl—but words. Directed at Evie.

"WHAT IS THIS AWFUL BODY YOU HAVE PUT ME IN?"

Evie staggers back. She reaches for an aisle seat to steady herself. I see her hand tremble. "My master! Ghazt. I—I'm sorry. It is a—ahem—*rat*. It's a type of rodent. It's, um—it's like the

Face is part rat and part melted plastic—it's barforama gnarly!

coolest animal on Earth. . . ."

"NOPE!" I shout. "EVERYONE HATES RATS!"

Ghazt glances my way. I shut up. His head swings back toward Evie. "WHY DID YOU BRING ME INTO THE BODY OF THIS ANIMAL? YOU ARE NOT WORTHY OF WORSHIPING REŻŻOCH!"

"I am sorry!" she cries. "I didn't mean to disappoint you! It's these lousy kids—"

Ghazt snarls, "YOU DID! AND YOU WILL PAY!"

June whispers, "Dudes, I think that's definitely our cue to leave."

I get Dirk's left arm over my shoulder. June slips underneath his right. The brand-new weapon gift around her wrist keeps Dirk steady.

And as Ghazt continues to scream and scold Evie, the failed villain, we race from the theater, out into the hall. . . .

The energy, the black lightning—it has brought new power and electricity to the theater. Every movie theater door is open. We hear bits and pieces of movies. The 20th Century Fox theme drums. Dialogue from some action-comedy trailer.

And worst of all . . .

Zombies. They are shambling out into the halls.

The water is pee-warm around our feet, like racing through a kiddie pool.

Angry, soul-shaking howls chase us down the hallway.

"This way!" I shout as we turn the corner. We all tumble and slide down the watery escalators. I feel tremendous heat in the air as we turn toward the massive, old-fashioned staircase that leads to the lobby.

I take three steps down, then stop.

The raging energy has melted the ice that was keeping the zombies *stuck*. The undead are free! The lobby is fully loaded!

More come stumbling out of the bathroom. They stagger in from the arcade.

Dirk hangs over our shoulders. His face is pale, almost see-through, and, to be honest, *freaking me out.* I totally know you're not supposed to judge people by how they look and that's, like, 110 percent a true and smart thing, but—man—looking at your almost-undead buddy is HARD.

Quint says, "He has to eat the eyeball innards!"

"I know, I know!" I say.

We're surrounded and trapped by horror. A zombie horde in front of us and a monstrous Cosmic Terror just one floor above us. But nothing is more urgent than Dirk eating the insides of that eyeball.

I glance down at it. No time to crack it open like a coconut and start feasting. Need a quicker solution. . . .

My eyes focus on the spinning Blue Raspberry ICEE sign behind the concession stand. I love those slushy slurpie drinks. . . .

And on the counter: a big thing of straws.

"THIS WAY!" I shout, and then we're racing down the steps. We are speeding *into* the arms of the enemy. Our feet splish-splash across the soggy floor. I dive over the glass popcorn box top first, then drop to the other side.

"Get back here!" I cry. I reach up, grabbing Dirk by the wrist, pulling him as June and Quint lift and push.

We collapse beyond the counter. It's our cover. The zombies march toward us from all sides.

And I think—y'know—Dirk would like this. It's like a Western. Impossible odds. Surrounded by an endless army of bad-dude, black-hatted cowboys. Or something. I dunno—I like sci-fi!

I look at June and Quint. I see the fear on their faces. On Dirk's face—eh, no fear, just creepy ghoul stuff.

June says, "Dirk needs to suck some eyeball."

"I'm on it!" Quint says.

Quint begins peeling the eyeball like it's a delicate tangerine or something. "No, Quint!" I say. "There's no time for gentle peeling!"

I grab a bendy straw and—

And then, the zombies are on us! Reaching over the counter! Grabbing and pawing! It's a full-blown terror-dome situation.

I hear a loud slurping as Dirk begins to drink. I look at June. And even as the zombies come closer and closer, there's this feeling. This feeling like maybe we *might* be OK here.

Because a devious, action-hero smile flashes across June's face. "Jack," she says. "I'm going to enjoy this gift. . . ."

She raises her arm, flexes her wrist again, and it *fully comes to life*. Every gadget pops out—every last thing. . . .

June's eyes narrow. "Merry Christmas, monsters. . . ."

THE GIFT THAT KEEPS ON BLASTING!

"It's working!" June shouts, as a *snap-bang* eruption flings four zombies backward.

But then there's a tremendous quake above us. Bits of ceiling dust flitter down. Suspended from the high ceiling is a tremendous sign that says POPCORN & SNACKS. Huge plastic block letters in an Indiana Jones sort of adventure font.

The whole thing rattles.

And then another tremendous quake. A monstrous footfall.

"Not good!" Quint screams. "It's Ghazt, above us. He's too heavy!" As Quint says that, the massive lettering falls. . . .

"WATCH OUT!" I shout.

We dive to the edge of the concession stand, away from the big inner circle of popcorn machines and extra candy storage.

KRAKA-SLAM!

It feels like thunder behind us. I'm slammed against a glass counter. I see Dirk tumble forward. The straw is knocked from his mouth.

His hand opens.

His fingers stretch out.

It's like it happens in slow motion. Like a runaway bomb in a movie. . . .

The eyeball rolls across the floor. It slips beneath the legs of the crowding zombies. Out into the theater lobby.

I look at Dirk. Quint shakes his head. "He hadn't finished it," he says.

I want to run out and grab the eyeball—but I can't even *see* it now. Because the zombies have fully closed in. We squeeze, huddling together. But they're coming.

Over the counter.

Onto us.

Well... At least it's a cinematic ending....

chapter twenty-three

The zombies are on us! Quint's robes are shredded! Teeth sink into June's shoulder pads! A dripping mouth on Quint's wrist. Hands tearing open my big white puffy pants.

This is it.

At last, it's happened—we have been overrun by the undead.

But then—

The air turns hot. A blast of energy fills the lobby. There's a hollow sound—I don't quite *hear* it, but I feel it in my eardrums, and suddenly—

The zombies are *flung* backward on their heels! It's like they're being yanked by invisible strings!

I look at my friends. June nods—she's OK.
Quint, too—he's all right. I check myself—no
zombie bites! Some damaged gear—but that's it!

"Hey," I say. "Winter action suits to the rescue!
THEY SAVED US!"

Another blast of energy, and I hear zombies
being thrown against the far walls. I peek over
the side, and see—

235

Warg told us Ghazt could control the
zombies—and man oh man, she wasn't kidding.
The zombies continue to move *backward*. It's
like watching a movie of zombies swarming, but
played in rewind. I can almost hear the reverse
vrap-vroot-vwoop noise.

Soon, the undead humans form a perfect
circle around the perimeter of the lobby. It's
five zombies deep, like a school dance, gathered
around the action.

Ghazt takes another step, his front paw
hitting the wet lobby floor.

236

And that's when I see it.

The eyeball, right there in the middle of the lobby.

"Quint, June—I'm going for the eyeball. It's Dirk's only chance."

I spring up, leaning over the counter, eager.

Evie notices me. And she looks down and sees the eyeball, at her feet.

"You want this, huh?" she shouts. Then she leans down and picks it up. "You can have it—*if you protect me!*"

My eyes narrow. I feel June's hand on my shoulder.

I look at Dirk. The straw in his lap. His eyes are foggy. He's cold and shivering and I just want to help him.

I hoist myself over the counter. I try to do it in a cool, smooth way—like an action hero sliding across the hood of a car—but instead I bang my knee, trip, and stumble.

Water splashes against the Louisville Slicer. I'm not sure, but I think I hear the blade and water sizzle. . . .

"Evie," I say. "Throw me the eyeball or I'm not taking another step toward you."

Evie thinks. Hesitates. Then does.

I don't catch it.

Quint does.

And in a flash, Dirk has his lips back on the straw, sucking out that remaining gooey eyeball goodness.

I stride across the squishy carpeting. I feel Ghazt watching me as I step in front of Evie. The chorus of the moaning zombies is in full surround sound.

Ghazt's strange, animal eyes narrow. Taking me in. Getting to know me. And I do the same.

MOVE, BOY. YOU ARE NOT MY ENEMY. YET. . . .

My muscles are tense. My knees are shaking. I'm sure Ghazt sees my fear—but still—I won't let this monster have the human.

"I can't," I say.

The monster's rat-like tail coils and sways. Ghazt steps closer. "SHE IS YOUR FOE."

"Yes." I nod. "But . . . But—well I don't know the but, really—I just know that I can't let you, like, eat her. Or whatever."

His rodent lip curls into a snarl. He looks me up and down—then focuses on the Louisville Slicer. "SO THIS IS THE ARTIFACT, YES? IT HAS SLAIN A COSMIC SERVANT? IT DOES NOT LOOK LIKE MUCH. . . ."

And at that moment, with a sudden snarl—

Ghazt's rat-tail snaps, and his jaws are gnashing, and he's lurching forward, and—

SLICE!

The blade cuts through the monstrous whisker like a hot knife through butter. Half a whisker drops to the floor.

I see the blade glow *black*.

Ghazt recoils.

"Um, look—I'm really sorry," I say. "I hope you weren't, like, too attached to that big whisker. I mean, well, obviously, you were *attached* to it because it was jutting out of your face, so—poor choice of words. My bad. I meant—"

"REARRRRCH!" The great rat monster howls and leaps at me.

"Ahh!" I cry out as I begin to flee. "I'M SORRY! I just meant, like, probably the whisker doesn't mean a whole lot to you! You've only had whiskers for, like, seven minutes, so . . ."

"Jack, shut up and watch out!" June shouts from behind the counter. "PAW!"

I duck as Ghazt's massive claws slice through the air. "THANKS, BUDDY!"

My feet are splish-splashing as I race around the lobby. It's not easy to outrun a giant monster when you're trapped inside a ring of the undead. One zombie tugs at my shoulder. My ankle rolls, and I stagger into the middle of the arena.

Just then, Ghazt's paw comes at me, and—

I'm sailing into the zombies' arms, but then—
WHOOSH!

Ghazt's mind-powers *hurl* the zombies aside,
clearing a path for me. I *slam* into the big mix-
your-own-soda machine. A dozen spouts of
flavor erupt. Grape. Cherry vanilla. Orange
stuff. Bubbling soda water rains down on me
like a sticky shower.

It rains down on the Louisville Slicer.

241

The blade sizzles. Steam rises.

Ghazt's eyes flicker over the Louisville Slicer.

Something about it—it causes him to hesitate.

The monster rat's thick, gray hair stands on end. Its strange, melted plastic features ripple.

I realize: He's frightened.

The Louisville Slicer—it scares him.

And whatever scares Ghazt, it scares me, too. Because, I see that it has changed.

It is dark and burnt. Even through my gloves, I feel that the handle is hot. It's like it's radiating an energy I don't understand.

"I don't totally get what's happening here," I say. "And I don't know what evil stuff you plan to get up to. But I do know this: My friends and I are going to do everything we can to stop you."

And with that—I swing.

The air swirls. Winds snaps.

Black energy streaks off the blade. A wide, ebony arc hangs in the air, and I smell smoke and fire.

Ghazt's tail switches. He snarls, then rears back, shrieking, and—

My hands tremble. The Louisville Slicer is *different*. It has some new power because of what happened. I lift the blade—and Ghazt recoils again. I lift it higher, and the zombies *jerk* like a jolt of electricity went through them.

Ghazt suddenly looks weak and drained. It's like the full force of the interdimensional summoning is suddenly hitting him all at once.

He looks to Evie. "SOMETHING IS NOT RIGHT."

"I—I am sorry," she mumbles.

He sags into the water. "I SHOULD DESTROY YOU FOR THIS OUTRAGE."

There is a calm, quiet moment as—for the first time—this Cosmic Terror truly examines his surroundings and the place to which he has been called. Ghazt lifts a paw. Eyes it.

He looks around the broken theater—and then through the shattered windows—at the crumbling end-of-the-world landscape.

And then, finally, back at Evie. "YOU ARE LUCKY. YOUR DESTRUCTION IS DELAYED—FOR THE MOMENT. THIS WORLD IS NEW TO ME. MY BODY IS WEAK. THERE IS SOMETHING STRANGE AT PLAY. YOU WILL HELP ME."

"I will?" Evie asks.

"YES. NOW TAKE ME AWAY FROM HERE. AWAY FROM"—he

pauses to eye me, my friends, and the Louisville Slicer—"AWAY FROM THIS. . . ."

Evie stands there for an awkward moment. She looks the huge creature up and down. "Um, *take you*. Right. I'll just—I can try to, um . . ."

She grabs his tail, pulls. Doesn't work. She puts a shoulder into his side, tries to push—grunts, fails. If it were not the most insane thing I'd ever seen, I'd laugh.

Gasping, she says, "General, you are a little large. . . ."

The monster's coiled tail flicks. Warm air rushes over me. Then—

WHOOMP!

The same noise—that same blast of energy in the air. Hollow. I whirl, horrified, as the zombies all come stumbling forward. Evie eyes me— suddenly very proud of herself.

The zombies all act *together*. The entire crowd of the undead, in unison, grabs hold of him. They lift—and their moans are strange and thunderous. His army carries him out, through the shattered front of the cinema.

Evie stands, watching Ghazt. "Can I ride you?"

Ghazt snarls. "NO! RETRIEVE MY WHISKER!" he shrieks at Evie.

"*Then* can I get a ride?" Evie asks.

"BRING! THAT! STUPID! WHISKER! YOU FOOL!"

"Sorry, General! Yes, General!" She quickly scoops up the whisker and chases after him. The army of the undead carries Ghazt off, through the white slush, into the distance. The last thing I see, through the horde, is Evie. She looks back and catches my eye. And she smiles a foul smile. . . .

She smiles because she *won.* The Cabal of the Cosmic has prevailed.

For the first time, my buddies and I straight-up lost. We stopped nothing. Prevented nothing. Saved nothing.

A loud SLUUUURP sound causes my head
to jerk toward the concession stand. It's Dirk,
sucking the straw—sounds like that last bit of
a milkshake. "HEY, BUDDY. YOU OK?!" I shout
out as I hurry over.

He looks tired, his eyes all dazed and foggy,
but his head lifts.

Dirk nods, smiles, then his face twists. He's
looking at the shriveled eyeball in his hand.
"Guys . . . did I just, um, suck out of the inside of
this thing?"

Quint grins. "Indeed you did!"

Dirk thinks about that for a moment. Then he
says, "Cool."

I was wrong. We did stop *something*. We did save *someone*.

Our friend.

And for now, that's enough.

Just then—loud paws! Rover, nudging Snow Mama toward us.

"The Big Mama Sled," Dirk says. "You found it? Oh. So you—so you saw my card. You know—I can't go with you. To New York."

There's a long, still silence.

Just a month earlier, we fought to get in touch with other humans. And the radio signal beckoned people—anyone—to New York City. But that seems like so long ago. . . .

That was before we knew there were humans who knew about Ŗeżżőcħ and Ghazt and Cosmic Terrors. Now nothing seems safe. I mean, it's not like I think there's necessarily a big group of Ŗeżżőcħ lovers hiding inside the Statue of Liberty, waiting to ambush us. But it's more like—like I can only *really* trust what I *know*. And I *know* my friends. And that's about it.

Quint says, "I won't be going, either. We are the only ones who know about Ghazt's arrival. There is now a new darkness. There is an enemy. He is wounded. But for how long?"

I realize I've been looking at the floor this whole time. I lift my head—and I look at June. A tear is rolling down her cheek. I swallow— and I say one of the hardest things I've ever had to say. . . .

June, I'll still go with you. Together, we can finish what the radio call started. The hope that maybe that's where we can get in touch with your family.

No, Jack. I'm not crying because Dirk and Quint aren't going. I'm crying because I can't go either. Not anymore.

There's something bigger than us going on here. We can't leave until it's finished. . . .

That hangs in the air. We didn't ask for it, but we're part of something now. Something huge. Something greater than even, like . . .

"Christmas!" June exclaims, leaping to her feet. "It's officially Christmas!"

"We barely got any gifts . . ." I say. "But—we can bring dessert home! Look at all the movie candy here! Let's grab some boxes and throw them into the sled. I mean, it *does* kind of have a Santa vibe right now."

And soon . . .

We return to town like triumphant, gift-giving Christmas heroes! We rode around— stopping off to get Dirk something to drink (mainly to wash the taste of eyeball from his mouth) and to snag some last-minute presents. It's snowing as we ride in. Heavy flakes pound the town, but the monsters aren't scared anymore.

They're just happy to see us.

Bardle pulls me aside. "You are OK. . . ." He sort of says it but it also sounds like he's asking it.

I nod. "I am. We are. But Ghazt? Man, things are *serious*. And big. Big things are coming."

"I assumed that much," he says. "We have much to do. Your world grows unstable. Tilted on the axis."

Riiiight. Yeah, that sounds bad. But before we address that, Dirk staggers over. He stumbles into me, laughing, throwing his arm around me. He's happily downing the thickest mug of hot chocolate I've ever seen.

He's happy.

Overjoyed.

I guess that's the look of a kid who got bitten by a zombie, went like 99 percent zombie, and then got yanked back from the brink of undeadness.

It's a big smile.

"Hey!" he suddenly exclaims. "We never did *my* Christmas tradition!"

"What was it?" June asks. She and Quint are bopping over, eating beef jerky.

"We must do it now!" Quint says.

"Christmas *king of the hill battle*!" Dirk says. "I had been thinking it would just be me up on the top mound, taking on every last breathing being. But ya know—I kinda want you three by my side."

Quint, June, and I all grin—and moments later, we're standing atop the Town Square's most massive snow mound. Dirk has his back to mine. June and I are shoulder to shoulder. Quint's breathing beside me.

And something about it—

I start giggling. Quint gets it, too, the giggles. And June is flat-out hysterical as we're all up there, feeling good, alive, with Dirk screaming "BRING IT ON!"

Our monster buddies charge. As I wait for them to reach us, I see a flicker in the distance. Christmas candles, being lit.

It's the Christmas tree farm.

Warg.

She got into the spirit. Maybe she'll make her way down here. Or maybe we'll go visit her. We do owe her a gift. Something *good*. Because she got us the best, biggest gift of all.

Dirk.

The big lug.

The big lug who orders us to "BRACE YOURSELVES!" as we try not to laugh any harder as the monsters are upon us. . . .

THE END!
(for now . . .)

Acknowledgments

As always, the most tremendous thank you to Douglas Holgate for bringing my vague notes and imprecise ideas to beautiful, stunning, monstrous life. Leila Sales, my steadfast editor—I can't thank you enough. Jim Hoover, for designing, designing, re-designing, then designing some more. You are so appreciated. Bridget Hartzler, my kick-butt publicist who kicks butt at kicking-butt—you rock. To Abigail

Powers, Krista Ahlberg, and Marinda Valenti—thanks for keeping the series typo-free. Erin Berger, Emily Romero, Carmela Iaria, Christina Colangelo, Felicity Vallence, Kim Ryan and everyone else in Viking's marketing and publicity department—thank you for your belief in this series and for taking it to the next level, again and again. And it goes without saying: Ken Wright, for every last thing. Robin Hoffman and all the folks at Scholastic, for your endless support. Dan Lazar, at Writers House, for oh so many things—too many to mention. Cecilia de la Campa and James Munro, for helping Jack, June, Quint, and Dirk travel the world. Torie Doherty-Munro, for always being patient and answering my annoying calls! And Addison Duffy and Kassie Evashevski, for helping take this beyond. Matt Berkowitz—thank you for your endlessly helpful notes, thoughts, and for reading and reading when you already have so much other, better reading to do.

And my wonderful family: Alyse and Lila. You make it all worthwhile.

MAX BRALLIER!

(maxbrallier.com) is the *New York Times* bestselling author of more than thirty books and games, including the Last Kids on Earth series. He writes both children's books and adult books, including the Galactic Hot Dogs series and the pick-your-own-path adventure *Can YOU Survive the Zombie Apocalypse?* He has written books for properties including *Adventure Time, Regular Show, Steven Universe, Uncle Grandpa,* and *Poptropica.*

Under the pen name Jack Chabert, he is the creator and author of the Eerie Elementary series for Scholastic Books as well as the author of the *New York Times* bestselling graphic novel *Poptropica: Book 1: Mystery of the Map.* Previously, he worked in the marketing department at St. Martin's Press. Max lives in New York with his wife, Alyse, who is way too good for him. His daughter, Lila, is simply the best.

Follow Max on Twitter @MaxBrallier.

The author building his own tree house as a kiddo.

DOUGLAS HOLGATE!

(skullduggery.com.au) has been a freelance comic book artist and illustrator based in Melbourne, Australia, for more than ten years. He's illustrated books for publishers such as HarperCollins, Penguin Random House, Hachette, and Simon & Schuster, including the Planet Tad series, Cheesie Mack, Case File 13, and *Zoo Sleepover.*

Douglas has illustrated comics for Image, Dynamite, Abrams, and Penguin Random House. He's currently working on the self-published series Maralinga, which received grant funding from the Australian Society of Authors and the Victorian Council for the Arts, as well as the all-ages graphic novel *Clem Hetherington and the Ironwood Race,* published by Scholastic Graphix, both co-created with writer Jen Breach.

Follow Douglas on Twitter @douglasbot.

A monster-sized thanks to everyone who pre-ordered *The Last Kids on Earth and the Nightmare King!*

Drew D.	Zachary B.	James M.	Kevin L.
Robert "RJ" C.	Hailey C.	Payten B.	Noah B.
Sophia F.	Nicolas B.	Delaney O.	Lucy F.
Jovaughn F.	Ethan J.	Landon M.	Sean Colin D.
Loki B.	Everett S.	Logan W.	Lupita S.
Diego F.	Carson O	Sean Ethan D.	Oliver S.
Benicio M.	Candido S.	William H.	Trinity M.
Andrew M.	Jacob P.	Kaiden F.	Alysse Z.
Dominic A.	Gavin A.	Laken R.	Ison S.
Brody M.	Jack B.	Cason T.	Draven S.
Nate K.	Keegan R.	Braelynn Z.	Brant L.
Sam O.	Brady M.	Cassidy M.	Lucas F.
Jake O.	Zeke R.	Gabriel R.	Demitri F.
Tyler S.	Toby R.	Connor M.	Beckett L.
Onyx G.	Aidan F.	Kailea B-J	Zackarey M.
Elijah H.	Odin B.	Rowen B-J	Landon J.
Logan M.	Trey M.	Grant W.	Chayse H.
Ty B.	John M.	Rielly J.	Cooper L.
Cyrus R.	Jackson W.	Isaiah M	Daniel K.
Riley M.	The Napier Boys	Nathan S.	Phoenix P.
Constantine B.	Nicolas L-S.	Andrew H.	Zoe B.
Spencer P.	Declan E.	Kenneth S.	Dyllan M.

Keegan N.	Logan T.	Dawson U.	Henry G.
Alex L.	Hayden M.	Adrian W.	Connor K.
Ethan P.	James C.	Ajax O.	Colton B.
Flint H.	Braxton M.	Tristan L.	Noah R.
Ben M.	Nia M.	Hunter K.	Adam D.
Korrine C.	Logan M.	Hartford B.	C.J. L
Lillian H.	London M.	Ziggy B.	Raya E.
Mason C.	Blake A.	Caden N.	Reagan R.
Andrew H.	Olivia M.	Zoe N.	Duke A.
Eli F.	Connor A.	Cadden K.	Brayden R.
Scotty L.	Lydia H.	M'Kenzie M.	BWE Bulldogs
Lukas B.	James R.	Dirk W.	Logan G.
Sadie S.	Logan G.	Sachi G.	Garrett W.
Bradie D.	Zeke Y.	Ezra B.	Ryan P.
Isaac A.	Brandon S.	Kade R.	William E.
Garrett S.	Andrew T.	Daniel A.	Anders O.
Cade E.	James M.	Andy R.	Nolan B.
Rylee S.	Liam K.	Michael C.	James H.
Kasey C.	Jack A.	Gabriel L	Braiden G.
Grant G.	Owen M.	Jesus A.	Max W.
Riya P.	Easton S.	Jackson H.	Evan M.
Cole S.	Oakley P.	Ryan N.	Chance L
Maxwell VB.	Jesus A.	Bryte C.	Julian A.
Marionni M.	Noah R.	Gavin L	Aaron H.
Ansh P.	Kason H.	Braeden C.	